ONCE UPON A WANING STAR

A Literary Chronicle of America at the Edge of Time

A Novel by

R. LUCE

ISBN: 979-8-9922202-0-9 (Hardback)
ISBN: 979-8-9922202-1-6 (Paperback)
ISBN: 979-8-9922202-2-3 (Digital)

Cover design and layout by Veronica Scott
Cover art from *Adobe Stock* images.

For John

Acknowledgements

Thank you to the professional reviewers from Book-Life and Reedsy for their comments and appreciation of the book. I am indebted to Veronica Scott for her commitment to creating cover and interior design that serves my readers, but which also expresses my personal tastes and artistic vision. I am also indebted to Rodney Hatfield for his wisdom and advice and for educating me about promotion and marketing. A special thank you to John Cunningham who puts up with me on a daily basis.

1

It has been two years since it started: the writing of a play that now becomes a not-play, a splash of not-quite black words upon the light gray of my computer screen, word sounds roiling in the openings of my ears and cascading over rocks of meaning and rushing into my brain's caverns before I can catch them, examine them, claim them. My eyes are heavy. My body is tired, has been for a long time: too much work, too little sleep—an unconquerable and relentless problem.

When I try sleeping, voices of my creations talk: Brad, Kevin, Matt, among them. They want to know what they are supposed to be doing, what is the point of their existence, and what will become of them when I am done with them. Sometimes, when they're tired of talking about their problems, they talk about what I have given them to think about: they rail against the ugliness that has become America, the derailing of the ideals that once held us together, the rise of blatant greed and lust for power. The loss of kindness. The end of this thing we call a republic.

The end of hope, for which we cling to one another and weep.

It's not easy spending time with these people. I try to convince myself that they are better than other voices competing for my attention—the divisive voices of misogyny, racism, homophobia ... all forms of hatred. Then, there are the voices of my literary progenitors who constantly demand that I find more of me than I have ... or more accurately, more than I've been able to find in myself thus far. It feels to me sometimes that there is an unnamed something I am expected to discover hiding in a brown-grocery-bag-wrapped package hidden behind a locked door in some unused room within the folds of my brain. If there is such a space down a hallway on a floor of the multi-tiered, multi-roomed gray mass of my brain, I haven't found it. An architectural drawing of the space I inhabit in my head would be helpful, but if I ever had one, I must have lost it somewhere along the many roads of my life experiences.

As if I didn't have enough distractions related to trying to be a writer, I have to deal with the voice of negativity always ready to toss a bomb into what little confidence I have. It is merciless, knows every trick for using my own self-doubts and fears against me: "You aren't good enough ... never will be," "Nobody cares about what you have to offer," and many other quite disturbing statements that I try to over-talk with ego statements, "Why not?" "You lie!" "Shut up!" "I'm doing it anyway!" and "The worst that can happen is it's a flop, and it's my flop to make!" But there is a worst. I can lose the ability to fight back and can be convinced they are right and fall into days, weeks, or months of debilitating depression

I like looking at things from different points of view when I am clear headed enough to understand them, and I like having to rethink what I previously thought I meant—sometimes having to rearrange my world around new ways of thinking. I just wish the discordant voices of my imagination would come at me one at a time instead of their usual trick of talking all at once.

Of course, I know the voices are my own, my way of trying to figure out what I want to do with plot and character for readers through the art of saying versus the skill of putting words together in coherent sentences, but art, like a hummingbird, is difficult to catch. It hovers above words but depends upon them for their nectar even as it demands a life of its own.

When I am at my best, I think of art as a way of being and becoming, and if I am fortunate, others will like what I have to say. Some people seem to think of art as a means for an artist to gain some kind of fame, fortune, and immortality. I toyed with these ideas long ago, but came to think of them as silly concepts, a self-aggrandizing fantasy that rots in the ground beside the carcasses of its believers. Notoriety and riches have eluded me, and I have eluded them, and I think that best. For me art is about living my brief moments upon this planet as honestly as I am able and making things that go beyond the utilitarian and that attempt to answer, "Why?" My time is spent in trying to understand who I am and who we humans as a species are beneath the façades we show to one another—the good, the bad, and the downright ugly, our self-delusions and the mental constructs created for us through coercion and judgments of others—that which we call "culture"—"others" telling us who we are, were, might be, and should be, much of it steeped in mendacity. So many layers of lies lie between thick tungsten-skinned fears and self-loathing it seems to me, and, therefore, are much easier to deal with than truth. Truth is maddeningly difficult to find, and often, when we think we've found it, it escapes and becomes something else that later becomes something other than that.

As far as I am concerned, being an artist isn't so much about finding the truth as it is about seeking the truth and marking steps along the way to remind ourselves—and interested others—where we have been and maybe make it easier for the next person to pursue. It is also about trying to find something worth saying in some symbolic form—something that I can use as a touchstone to inspire me to carry on when I am discouraged by my fellow human beings (which is quite often). If others are find value in what I make, all the better; that's a gift for my ego, but I maintain that it must be irrelevant to the act of making art honestly.

This thing that I am about to create is a book-I-want-to-read-but-which-hasn't-been-written-so-I-have-to-write-it (a la Toni Morrison), and it frightens me. It's not my first attempt. The words, stories, and experiences behind it have written themselves into and out of existence like grocery lists over the past two years, yet my mind returns incessantly to the sounds and images that demand I write them as honestly as I am able before setting them before you. If you are reading this, it probably means they succeeded, at least for me, and I like the book I wrote.

2

Prologue

January 6, 2022

[Enter the Fool.]

A middle-aged man—Fool—carrying a bottle half-full of whiskey comes through a doorway pulling the door shut behind him before stepping tentatively into the faint blue light of the backstage of a theater. He is like a man set ashore by Charon at hell's entrance. He moves as though he is being pulled by the red-orange light of fate he sees in his mind's eye and by the sound of Hades' beautifully mournful song. He scrunches his eyes and cheeks, holds his shoulders high and tight, turns his neck and head from side to side as he puts one foot cautiously in front of the other as he tries to avoid tripping over something he cannot see. Guided by the ever-so-faint yellow light creeping in the side spaces between the stage curtain and the prosce-nium wall, he stops at the hand-lock device holding taut draw ropes stretched between the bolted casing's pulleys and the immense weight of the grand drape hanging upon the batten overhead. He grips the hard rasp-like skin of the rope, holds it as if to honor how much depends upon the multitudinous fibers and its stack of counterweights.

The man tries to remember how and by whom the Harlequin's hat has been placed upon his head, one of its prongs dangling a wooly ball just above his brow. He releases his grip on the rope to tuck the whiskey bottle between his knees, then reaches up, pulls the fool's crown off his head. He stares at it, studies the three floppy, conical shoots that burst from the band and that bend happily like thin-stemmed, bloom-heavy peonies. The hat turns round and round in his hands as he follows the diamond patterns of the hat's cloth: black diamond, white diamond, alternating, perpetual circles around the stems climaxing in red pompoms at the top. Black, white, red ... he assumes, though he knows that blue light tells lies about what the light of day says.)

FOOL: *[Looking at the hat.]* Thou art a flaccid trinity bowing before a Fool!

He squeezes his knees upon the whisky bottle which is beginning to slide from its thick belly to its neck and begins to fall; he lowers one hand to catch it, then sets it ever so gently like a child on the matte black floor—a floor made to kill light and swallow it whole. As he straightens, the bottle fades to black at his feet. Fearful that it might escape him, he bends over to feel for it, reassure himself that it hasn't moved. When he rises, he resets the fool's crown on his head and holds it in place as he squats to reach the bottle's neck and take it safely back in his hand like a Christmas goose in a Dickens' tale.

He stares into the barely visible space before him. Though he might not say it, he has long thought of this eerie necessity of staging as a sadness of lights grudgingly given. Blue light is meant to serve, prevent his or anyone's human propensity for self-destruction, destruction of property, and harm to one another—actors crashing into crew members standing in gloomy shadows or actors arriving out of the bowels of the building thoughtlessly to the call for "Places!" Until his eyes adjust, it is like awakening in a lightless bedroom, far from the light switch, and no one in the bed to cling to. As he waits for whatever is or isn't to come, he speaks softly in a Shakespearean dialect.

FOOL: A tittering tease of light, thou art, that leads us all-too-soon to sunlit fame ere thou taketh us into eternal night.

He holds the bottle belt-high on his waist, unscrews its cap, and takes a drink, then wipes his lips on his stained shirt sleeve. The act of dropping his head as it follows the bottle downward to its place on the floor causes one of the hat prongs and attached pom to drop. His first instinct is to catch the hat like a falling coin, but he is a whippet chasing a mechanical rabbit in a race it needn't run for a prize it will never get. He follows it downward, his whole body falling forward and to the floor. As he lifts himself up, his eyes catch a hint of white light sneaking through the minute space between the massive drape and the stage floor. It is a beckoning from the other side, the side where the people are—an evening's voyeurs waiting like him for whatever is or isn't to come. With his back against the stone and concrete of the proscenium wall, he takes hold of the thick, most-likely-red-or-blue-or-purple velvet curtain and pulls it back just far enough to see that there is a spotlight shining on the center of the wide drape he is holding. It is a light that makes an orb of rose ringed by shades of coral, orange, and red that deepens to maroon and burnt umber in the residual light escaping into the edges of blackness the Lekos, Ellipsoidals, and Fresnels have not yet lit. He steps away from the wall to stand behind the drape, using it to cover his body as he pulls it slowly, as unnoticeably as possible, far enough back for him to peak around its edge and look briefly into the house, hears an old admonition playing in his head: "If you can see them, they can see you!" But he cannot see beyond the blinding beam coming from somewhere high above the seating area. Releasing the drape slowly, he listens for subdued coughs, shuffling of feet, sounds of any life beyond himself. But there is nothing, no discernable sound, nothing but the spotlight waiting, nothing but him deciding what to do with the nothing he is in. He looks backstage once more, hoping someone comes into view who knows what to do, someone who can point him to an exit for an inconspicuous escape, or someone who will push him out onto the stage. Someone to do something. But there is no one beyond himself except for me, and I will not interfere.

FOOL: *[Speaking aloud to himself.]* Do something, Fool! Someone has to do something. People are waiting. Anything. Anything is better than nothing! Act!

The beating drum of self-abuse continues, raises his hackles, makes him want to lash out against it, "It's not my responsibility!"

And yet, he feels the presence of an audience waiting, growing restless. He is trying to make sense of this place, this strange *now* that he can't seem to turn away from and escape. He takes a slug of whiskey, looks back at the dark behind him, turns to the light, and as if pushed from behind, he sweeps the curtain back and steps onto the stage where he feels the sudden warmth of the spot on him. Uproarious applause, whistles, shouts, and stamping feet follow him and the spotlight as he makes his way to the center of the stage area—the apron—where he turns to face the blackness from which the sounds come. He shakes his head in an attempt to clear the effects of the alcohol, and then bows before the din of appreciation. He feels the pull of the sloshing bottle on his arm as he lowers it to the stage floor, hears it clunk briefly on the wood. He smells the odors that cling to his worn, wrinkled, and holey clothes and the odors of his unwashed and sockless feet showing through the rips and tears in his canvas shoes.

FOOL: *[Aside.]* They expect something from me; they think I know what to say, know what I am about to do, and why I am doing it. I don't.

He rises from his bow, lifting the bottle up with him as the applause, whistles, and shouts continue for a moment more and then fall to silence as he struggles for something to do with what he has to work with: his mind, body and his bottle. The whiskey weighs heavily in his hand; he looks at the label, "Maker's Mark." While unscrewing the bottle's plastic cap, he looks out into the black mass that has proclaimed its existence in a collective clinking, clunking, and clanging of human anonymity. The words, "Anything is better than nothing," rattle like ghosts in the many rooms of his brain until they coalesce to demand an action. He makes a cartoon-like smile, his mouth suddenly bigger, his teeth suddenly bigger and taking up half his face, his body somehow bigger and taking up space it hasn't taken prior to this moment. With his left hand he lifts the bottle and holds it two or three inches off to the left side of his face. Simultaneously, he raises his right-hand to just below his chin with his rigid pointer finger aiming at the bottle, listens to the laughter the gesture makes. He switches the whiskey to his right hand and thrusts the bottle forward to the phantoms filling the theater.

FOOL: Prost!

He pretends to drink deeply while holding his tongue against the rim to stop the free flow of the whiskey, allowing only enough of its liquid to get through to wet his tongue and coat his throat. Then he wipes his bottom lip and his chin on a grimy sleeve and waits for the house to quiet.

FOOL: *[Speaking directly to the audience.]* I'm feeling better. How about you? *[After a beat and a recognition of chuckles from the audience, he says,]* So ... What are you doing here? *[Again, he waits for the laughter to subside.]* Seriously. Who let you in here? I've been hanging out backstage for a while; haven't seen a soul. Hell, I don't even know who let me in here. I didn't know you were out here until just a minute ago. Ever feel like you're a puppet just hanging out in life waiting for someone to pick up the strings? That's how I feel right now.

I can't help but wonder if it is to me that he speaks. Or perhaps he seeks an answer to his emptiness from a phantom god he has conjured to save him from himself. As he ends the line, his whole body begins to move in herky-jerky fashion, his body parts attached to strings of imagination tied to a cross of wood. He is a Pinocchio imposter dancing in the spotlight amidst the roar of an approving crowd. At the moment just before the audience's laughter is fading, he steadies himself again and goes on assuming the role of a more confident self, a being from some past time when he could at least fake a laugh at himself and the inexorable loneliness that has become his life and about which he utters, only occasionally, words to an unnamed god.

FOOL: Most of the time, that's what I feel like: a dummy. I never know what's going on. This happens to me all of the time. I'm one place doing something, then I'm somewhere else doing something different. There I was a little while ago sitting in a nice quiet neighborhood bar ... well, really ... sitting on the steps outside the bar ... I think the bartender threw me out. So, I was sitting out there in the cold, in Ohio. Of all the goddamn places on earth anybody would ever think to be on a January night in 14-degree weather, that's where I was. Hell! Just minding my own business, and Poof! Here I am. By the way, where am I right now?

A VOICE: *[An echo of his own voice.]* You are still in hell, man!

FOOL: Ohio, Eh? Hell? You must be a Democrat! Oops! Probably shouldn't have said that. It's been like this my entire life, but it's gotten worse with age: Never knowing when I'm going to get dropped into something I'm totally unprepared for at the whim of some hack playwright. Don't even know what I'm supposed to be saying now. I'm making it up as I go. ... You're laughing. You think I'm joking. Okay, whatever. You'd think the ass who wrote whatever it is you're here for would have written some lines I could have rehearsed. No. I'm left flopping around out here on my own. Shakespeare never would have done that. He'd have me saying something worth saying even if I was saying it to some villain who is pulling the bloody sword out of my belly! Now, there's a guy who could write! Shakespeare! Remember this one? *[He strikes a noble pose.]* "To be, or not to be, that is the question." Probably the most important question ever asked, by the way. *[He relaxes his body, makes three snapping noises with the thumb and middle finger of his right hand, shifting his body from side to side—a 'cool cat' imitation of Sinatra before stopping to say,]* Some days I'm into Frank Sinatra's take on the subject; he was toasting someone at a party who was right around his own age and said jokingly, 'May you live to be

100, and may the last voice you hear be mine.' Other days, I'm with Redd Foxx of Sanford and Son fame" *[plays out the staggering movements of the TV show character pretending to be having a heart attack]* holding his chest, staggering around his living room, looking upward for heaven, and saying, "This is the big one! I'm dying! You hear that, Elizabeth! I'm coming to join you, honey!" *[After mimicking Sanford, he drops his free hand from his chest and goes on.]* Another one of my Shakespeare favorites, and the one that really hits home for me is this one; I'm sure you know it: *[He again strikes a noble pose and presents dramatically.]*

All the world's a stage,
And all the men and women merely players;
They have their exits and their entrances,
And one man in his time plays many parts ...

I mean, is that the sum of it all, or what? It's true, you know. We're all players. The only issue is whether we get stuck with endless bit parts or get to play a big juicy role every now and then. And a whole lot of that depends on whether or not the director likes your looks or your ass; to hell with your talent. It's a racket. Old Will was a pretty smart guy. Why doesn't anybody write like that anymore? The man was always getting at powerful stuff. He would have a field day with what's been going on here—the big "here" as in our time and place—right now—with what we've been going through. At any rate, here we are, you and me, and we don't even know why we're here. At least I don't. Does anybody know what's going on? Are we supposed to be here for a play? If we are, does anybody know what it's called ... the plotline ... anything at all? I sure as hell hope you don't think I can keep you entertained for an hour and a half! Come on, you must know something, or you wouldn't have wasted your money to get in here. Or are you as lost as I am? All of us at once? *[Pause.]* These writers! I tell you. I've had to put up with lots of them, been dragged into so many goofy plots. And always playing the fool or some version of one. Do I look like a fool to you? Never mind. Don't answer that. I forgot about the hat. I'm going to assume there is a play going on here tonight since you are out there, and the spotlight is on me up here and it's following me around. If it isn't a play, and nobody's coming out here to take my place, we've got no reason to be here, right? I'm running out of material, can't dance for beans, and believe me, you don't want to hear me sing, especially acapella—can't find a key to stick to from one note to the next. One thing I can do is make up a story. How about I make up a story? You okay with that? Yeah? Okay. Here goes: Once upon a time ... by the way, why is it that so many stories start 'once upon a time? What's wrong with telling about right now? We've got stories going on in the here and now, don't we? I've got one going on about me trying to figure out why the hell I'm here, but we already talked about that one, so I'll come up with a new one." He bows his head for a moment, pulls his free hand up to his chin, his fingers sliding up to the edge of his bottom lip. *[After a moment, he says,]* Okay, I've got it! *[He speaks rapidly but clearly.]* In a mythical land thousands of people were standing outside in the January cold and waiting. They had been waiting all morning, many of them holding their places in a too-long line to get into a theater that likely wasn't going to open a moment before the advertised time ... *[he slows down the speed of his speech]* people freezing be damned. *[Speeds up again.]* Others were waiting too, but they had no intentions of entering like cattle down a chute and were content to see images on huge outdoor screens and hear whatever words might eventually be said through the speakers fastened to the structure's exterior walls. They were waiting for reasons all their own. Some appeared to be military types. Most did not. Many were out-of-shape, non-descript men and women flapping their arms across their chests to stay warm; their bodies were rocking back and forth to keep their joints from freezing up. Each of them was defiant of the cold as if freezing made a statement all its own. When the theater's wide double doors opened at last, the people who had been waiting in line like hungry soldiers at the mess hall pushed all discipline aside to break into the space as fast as possible to get some heat and to find the best places to sit and eat the popcorn and cheese puffs they brought with them—seats preferably as close to the proscenium as possible. They had come for the show that is their king, to hear him: Fatpants the First—the merchant king who had invited them, the select of his kingdom. There was no playbill. It didn't matter. Whatever was done in his name was enough. The lights went out. *[He drives the following words forward, gaining speed and volume, building to a crescendo at the word "gong."]*A set of Timpani—large bowl and small bowl—began to pound out a rhythm that moved from a series of single beats to a faster rhythmical pattern of five beats alternating between the two drums and then becoming a drum roll on the large bowl which grows in intensity until the drumstick was lifted away and only the reverberations carried over into the clash on a huge brass gong. *[Returns to his previous speed and volume.]* Then the sound of the curtain being pulled made the audience sit upright as the lights faded up on a simple, cartoon-like representation of a village. What the audience was about to see was a version of what is called *commedia dell'arte*, not that anybody had used those words. "Slapstick" or "skit" was more likely the more palatable name the people would use to describe it to their friends when they finally got home. Probably for the best not to call it what it was: some of them wouldn't have known how to pronounce it, maybe would have thought it "too highfalutin'" for their tastes, but—to be fair—maybe they just hadn't cared what it was called as long as it was fun and easy to understand; they hadn't come for theatre. They had come to hear old Pantaloon and had not known—and would not have accepted—that he too was but a character from the genre. This particular performance started off with three conquering heroes entering the stage. They might have been thought of as heroes, but they were also what I would refer to as loud-mouthed braggarts! The audience quickly learned that these so-called heroes recently returned from putting down a revolt that had arisen in many parts of the kingdom of Rebuplica. Apparently, some blackguards had declared their displeasure with the king's decrees and had launched attacks to defeat and remove him: King Fatpants the First. Fatpants had formerly been a huckster who, through the magic of a playwright's invention and many instances of deception, had gained the title of king of the realm with a few specific limitations placed on him. Fatpants had to deal with a powerful house of lords and with a council of the judiciary. The king, of course, didn't like this check on his power and plotted to kill each of the lords and judges off as soon as possible, but until that happened, he ignored them as much as he could, and looked forward to the day when the assassinations could commence. Shortly after the heroes got on the stage, actors portraying the populace started coming from behind the curtains and out of the wings. Their characters were excited and happy to welcome the heroes and asked them to tell of their conquests. The braggarts exclaimed, "We have conquered and made fools of our foes, deflowered their virgins, and cuckolded their men! We have whipped the arses of their warriors and left them whimpering as they cooled their afflictions in the troughs of horses."

(The Fool takes on different roles, announcing characters, playing them, and then shifting stage position to differentiate each. He sets the bottle down until he completes all of the roles.)

AS WOMAN: A woman asks, *[speaking falsetto]* Doth that make them horse's arses then?

AS HERO: One of the heroes responds, *[in an exaggerated hypermasculine voice.]* Aye, it doth. 'Tis pity I have for thirsty horses who then drink the arse-spiced water.

FOOL: The audience roared with laughter! They were a low-brow humor crowd.

AS YOUNG MAN: An awestruck boy asks one of the heroes, How didst thou defeat an army larger than thine own?

FOOL: As you can see, this troupe was really into using "thee," "thou," "thine," and such ... and let's not forget "arse" ... all those cool words ... a bit surprising considering the audience they were playing to ... but I'm digressing, aren't I? Sorry. So, anyhow, the response to the guy's question, "How didst thou defeat an army larger than thine own," was this:

AS HERO: *[The hero touches the boy's shoulder as if giving a "dad talk," again using the hypermasculine voice.]* Me Lad, it is said that a bull doth defeat a hundred flies with a single sweep of his tail. Tis true! And that we did with our armies. But it is also true that a great many bulls can be driven to madness by the loss of their tails. With that we made them mad ... mad as March hares!

FOOL: The boy wasn't catching on. Just as someone began to explain it, a man—skinny, homely, dressed like a fop ... you know what a 'fop' is, right? It's a guy who would be on many a gay guy's gaydar, except he—this particular fop—would have to lose layers of lace and face paint before any self-respecting gay guy would touch him. By the way, Commedia dell'arte didn't have a character called a fop, it's just the best word I can come up with right now. At any rate, this fop guy and his well-dressed and beautiful wife came walking onto the stage and into the crowd. The woman, seeing the handsome heroes, immediately began to flirt with them. One of the heroes picked up on the flirtation and walked as if in a trance to the woman, pushed the husband aside like he was a sheer curtain, took the woman by the waist and pulled her close to him, kissed her deeply and practically made love to her right there in front of her husband and the audience. The angry husband, half the hero's size, puts up his fists like a pugilist ... *[Fool puts up his fists and starts dancing like an overeager inexperienced boxer.]*... the fists coming out of his floppy lace cuffs, mind you. The hero turned to face the fop. *[The Fool stops dancing.]* And then, the fop punched the hero's midsection as hard as he could punch. *[The Fool pretends to be punching something.]* The punch had absolutely no impact on the great battle-worn hero. It was as if the fop had punched a two-inch thick steel plate, and his arm began to reverberate with the pain rushing into his body causing him to go rigid and vibrate like a cartoon character that had stuck its finger into a light socket. *[The Fool mimics a cartoon character, his arm frozen in front of him, his body goes stiff and then begins to twitch and shake as he experiences waves of pain and spins in a circle, almost falling down before he stops to continue the story.]* Okay! So! When he—the husband—the fop—was done with his antics, a street person came up to him and pointed to the fop's shoe, which, as you can guess, has supposedly gotten dirtied in the scuffle. So, of course, in the world of commedia dell'arte, the fop was obliged to bend over to clean the shoe before returning to the fight. As he bent over, he got kicked in the backside—the 'arse' if you will—by one of the characters. That kick drove him into the arms of the two braggart heroes who had been standing by enjoying the fop's humiliation. They simultaneously punched the fop in the nose and let him fall to his hands and knees; then, they kicked his arse all the way across the stage as he tried to crawl away from his tormentors as quickly as possible while squealing like a pig until he was booted off stage. A couple of guys in the crowd were angry about the way the heroes treated the man. They started flexing their skinny arms and posing like pugilists until the three so-called heroes stepped in front of them blocking them from the audience's view and pummeled the two men to the ground. When the huge men stopped and stepped aside, the three members of "The Fop Squad" team were scuffed up, naked except for knee-length women's underwear flapping about their legs. *[The Fool puts his hands over his crotch, scrunches his body up, lifts his leg as if trying to hide the laughter coming at the fops' humiliation. After a moment, he relaxes the comedic pose.]* Now, here's the really important part. Remember that everything I just told you is a prelude to what the audience had actually come for. When the applause for the comedic entertainment ended, the house went dark and stayed dark as the theme for *2001: A Space Odyssey* began ... very dramatic. At the point where the timpani, trumpets and French horns climax, a spotlight dropped its beam stage left. King Fatpants ... the First ... stepped from the wings into the spotlight that followed him as he moved about, the audience now standing, applauding, shouting all kinds of praise, whistling those two-fingers – halfway-down-their-throat whistles that pierce the eardrums of anyone within fifty feet of the ass who does it. They loved him. His rotund body was draped in finest cloth; his face glowed yellowish orange, the gold crown on his head held his coiffed hair perfectly in place. He was swollen with self-satisfaction coming from the effusive, almost-hysterical adulation of the people, many hoisting banners to express support for his reign. Amidst the thundering expressions of love hurdling against his ears, Old Pantaloon, playing Fatpants the First, raised his arms as a gesture of appreciation like a diva who had given a bravura performance worthy of historical note ... though he had done nothing at all. He strutted before the audience, held their clamor in his death grip until they could no longer sustain it. When they finally quieted, he spoke.

FATPANTS: *[Taking on an air of pomposity.]* Loyal subjects, I beseech thee to listen well, for our hour is at hand! Wickedness hath slithered into the muddled minds of our lords. This day, they prepare to take our crown and our fruits of war so nobly won. They say we broke the covenant with the whining hordes; thus, they prepare to anoint a lesser man an unworthy king. A lesser man! Barely a man! They intend to empower a scourge of a people, a despicable people worthy of nothing but god's eternal damnation, empower them to make decisions for themselves, believe what they like, claim equality with you—and even me—their superiors. I tell thee, that if we do not take up arms, infidels shall soon be given our lands and our fortunes ... taking all that we have fairly gained during our most benevolent reign—the greatest, most magnificent, of history's reigns. I tell thee, the ungrateful heathens and the lords have forsaken us! Insolent chaff! I shall not be forsaken! Nor shall thee or thine! I ask thee, "Wilt thou ride with me this day against the house of lords? And, wilt thou fight? 'Aye! Aye,' ye say. Aye, faithful subjects! This day we ride to glory, smite the traitorous lords, and retain our rightful reign, no matter our costs in money or in blood!

FOOL: As you can guess, the people in that audience had been getting worked up almost from the beginning of the king's speech. The meaning of the day's spectacle had begun to make sense to them. They were standing, cheering, yelling, "We are with you!"—all proclaiming their love and allegiance. That's when he said:

FATPANTS: Then let us ride!

FOOL: The people were cussing and making threats and demands upon the air in support of their beloved king. Those outside watching on the monitors and listening to the monstrous speakers hanging from the sides of the buildings were also ranting. Clubs, knives and other weapons people had brought with them started coming up out of pant legs and pockets, from underneath hats, out of lunch sacks and other bags people had brought. Pitchforks were pulled from behind trees and brush where they had been hidden. People inside the theater pushed one another forward to the exit doors, each wanting to enter the fray. Once outside, they moved as quickly as possible to catch up with the others who had already gained a quarter-mile lead on the road to where the House of Lords met. Off they went, looking for a fight, which, by the way, they couldn't possibly win despite the bloviation of old Pantaloon. Contrary to what he said, he and his ragtag army hadn't won the war at all ... he was an accomplished liar ... he hadn't even come close to winning; the opposing forces had defended themselves well and counterattacked effectively winning the war decisively. Pantaloon had sent his audience on a fool's errand, maybe destruction, needless death while he returned to his castle and slept.

(He opens the bottle and takes a long drink, wipes his mouth, and then proceeds.)

FOOL: As I said, Fatpants and his sycophants couldn't win then. And they didn't. The end, right? No! What's really weird is that when he lost, he didn't face consequences. He was let off the hook, as they say, allowed to try again another day as if all was forgiven, crimes of State swept under the rug. Fools! They had to know he would plot to regain his crown and seek revenge on those who had toppled him; it was only a matter of time; and until then, he would cause no end of trouble. So, what's the moral of the story? *[He takes another long drink, wipes his mouth, tries to kill time while he dreams up a moral.]* When you finally shed fat pants, be smart! Stick to your diet and throw away the pants you never intend to go back to!

(Groans and boos come up out of the house along with a few laughs.)

Hey! What did you expect? No script. Remember? I told you from the get-go I didn't know why I was here. My best guess is that we're in a rough draft of another tale told by yet another idiot signifying nothing. No offense ... you haven't been much help. *[He drinks again and again as he talks, becoming more obviously inebriated by the moment, struggling with words now, pausing in awkward places to catch the thoughts that want to escape him.]* As my mama always said, 'It is what it is, Fool.' Used to think ... you know, like 'Duh!' when people said it, but you know, damned if she wasn't right. People are the way they are. Life is what it is. Chance is chance. 'Takes a hell of a lot of time and effort to change 'is' to 'was' if you know what I mean. Luck- -some people are born with it; some of us can't find it with a flashlight in the dark or with a magnifying glass, a map, and a paid guide in the daytime. Maybe "It is what it is" is dumb but sometimes the best collection of words ever! I mean, think about it. If Shakespeare said those words, we would carve them on porticos of great buildings. The best *we* can do is scribble them on a restroom stall wall ... something to stare at when you've got nothing else to do but wait. I don't know. Guess it depends on what you make of it. But maybe that's the point! Everything kind of depends on what we make of it. I mean, ask yourself, "Is anything actually what people say it is?" Speaking of 'is,' you know this whole theatre thing ... it's just smoke, mirrors, and cardboard, right? All art's that way. Not in the thing. In what we make of the thing. You know what I mean? It's an *is* that makes you think it's *the* 'is', but *is*— big *IS* — is somewhere else. This "is" thing is making me dizzy. Maybe Shakespeare knew what he was doing after all when he didn't write it. I'm really tired. He opens his bottle again, this time taking a long drink that makes the liquid bubble in the bottle before he stops and screws its cap into place. He speaks. This bottle has gained weight. *[He looks at it again. There is only a small amount left.]* What the hell! *[He drinks the bottle dry, then throws it; it makes a hollow clunk on the stage floor and the sound of heavy glass rolling to a stop against the curtain. He is trying*

*to keep his eyes open, his body upright and can't maintain
it. He sags to the floor and lies down as if to sleep. After a
few seconds, his eyes open. He hears the deadly hush of
the audience.]* I'm sorry. Just joking.

*(With a great deal of effort and lack of coordination,
he gets back on his knees, then tries to stand. He cannot.
He tries to claim a noble stance like Hamlet's Claudius
on his knees praying, but he is unable to sustain it. The
whiskey has caressed his brain, rocked him like a baby
toward sleep—a baby fighting the idea, a baby wanting to
get free of the constraints of its mother's arms one more
time before giving in. He stares into the darkness, listens
to a somehow-altered silence—not the sound of a hushed
audience—but an unutterable emptiness, a hollowness of
a life badly spent, a loneliness waiting somewhere below
his chin as he tries to look down over his nose at something out there beyond the stage that cannot and will not
be seen.)*

[He speaks sheepishly. Drunk.] Are you there? Is anyone
out there?

*(Only the echo of his own voice returns from paint-peel-
ing plaster walls of an unexplainably familiar space. The
spotlight is gone. A dull light from behind his eyes brings
the room into view, shows the heaps of debris where the
seats had been, illuminates the stage apron beneath him
layered in dust and chunks of fallen plaster. He faces a cur-
tainless and empty proscenium lit in a meager gray light
coming from a broken window high above what were once*

fly rails and rigging. He reaches up to feel for the prongs of the hat that is no longer on his head.)

Goddamned writers!

[Exeunt the fool.]

***

How sharper than a serpent's tooth it is to have a thankless child!

William Shakespeare, King Lear, I. iv.

3

Dave's Place is the name of the play that I wrote before I started this "not-play." I knew when I wrote it,
it was risky, and I didn't care ... or at least I told myself I
didn't. Even as I wrote it, I doubted anyone would produce
it. Like my other work, it was probably too far outside the
safe clichés to be considered, and it didn't have the requi-
site number of roles for women (a la Bechdel-Wallace de-
cree)—in fact, no women appear in it at all except through
Dave's storytelling about them. This is not because I don't
like women, but because the story I wanted to tell is about
three men. The play deals with political issues related to
the January 6th insurrection and deals tangentially with
the menace of Covid. It was probably going to be a loser all
the way around for making money. But then, moneymak-
ing had never been the important thing about writing it.

Despite my fears about its acceptance, a version of my
script managed to make it as a finalist in an international
award competition. It didn't win, but the fact that it was
chosen from nearly 1,000 scripts as a finalist was enough

for me to hope the play had a future. However, after reciting my mantra of "Your loss, Chump" to the seemingly
endless rejections, I returned to my original thoughts: The
play was written because it had to be written, and there
had never been any guarantees that it would become more
than an ink-splattered stack of paper in a desk drawer that
someone would throw away or burn up in the fireplace after I die. "Better to have written and failed to find a kindly
reader than never to have written at all," I told myself and
chuckled at the clichéd form that came so easily into my
mind.

Funny how things work themselves out: fate fell like a
wall upon me, and I happened to be standing where the
empty window space landed amongst the brick and concrete crashing on the grass. A phone call. A desire to stage
the play, contracts, rehearsals, opening night, playbills in
the hands of audience members to read for filling time before the play begins:

CAST

Brad Michaels: Dave Singh

Brad Michaels has appeared in productions in New
York, Chicago, and London. He has been highly praised for
his performances as Hal in William Inge's *Picnic*; Biff in
Death of a Salesman; Brick in *Cat on a Hot Tin Roof*; Joe in
Sunset Boulevard; Hamlet with the London Shakespeare
Troupe; and many other major roles. He has performed for

film (Marcus in *Sunflower*; Julian in *Late Last Night*, and Everett in *Lost Cause*) and television ("Cranks" and "Livid."). Mr. Michaels was listed by *Entertainment News Magazine* as one of the top ten up and coming actors of 2021.

Kevin Lane: Jack Ingram

Kevin Lane's first major role was as Alan Strang in Peter Shaffer's *Equus* (San Francisco, 2017). Since that time, he has portrayed Tom Wingfield in a revival of Tennessee Williams' *The Glass Menagerie* (2019); Romeo in Shakespeare's *Romeo and Juliet* (New York production 2020); and Edmund Tyrone in Eugene O'Neill's *Long Day's Journey into Night* (Chicago production 2020). Over the past two years, Mr. Lane has performed on several television pro – grams and special project films.

Matt Connor: James Lathrop (a banker) and Bill Hagerty (a thug)

Matt Connor makes his return to Broadway for this production after a hiatus, performing two very different and difficult roles. He has performed in numerous stage productions, television programs and movies. Mr. Connor achieved great acclaim for his performances in Samuel Beckett's *Krapp's Last Tape*, and *Waiting for Godot*, New York productions of the Beckett Society of America; Shylock in *The Merchant of Venice*; Dodge in Sam Shepard's *Buried Child*; and many others.

SETTING: The play takes place in a bar in Pierlight, Ohio, a small city 70 miles southeast of Columbus. The action of the play occurs from late afternoon, January 7, 2021, until 1:30 a.m. January 8th. The Covid pandemic has caused businesses to struggle for survival; many have already closed their doors and accepted the loss of their livelihoods. It is the day after the insurrection—attempted coup—in Washington, DC. There is a fear that is spreading across the country that democracy itself is on the verge of collapse.

4

Backstage
October 8, 2021

[A theater in New York City.]

Brad Michaels sits at his dressing table and looks into his large mirror bedecked with lightbulbs along the top of the frame and down the two sides. Their brightness sucks the life out of the reverse image of the too-small dressing room, focusing everything on his own image staring back at him—an image that is him, but not him. It is the image the play demands and the patrons need. Every hair is in place. Carefully lined eyes, darkened eyelashes and brows will withstand the attempts by the hot lamps to hide his eyes from everyone sitting beyond the second row. Skin imperfections are hidden under a layer of "base cover" and blush matched to his particular skin color. Looking closely, he decides that there is a redness to his right cheek that is slightly stronger than that on his left; he tells himself that no one will be able to distinguish such a slight difference from a distance. He is right, of course, but he has noticed it and now it will be an annoyance, a distraction he doesn't want to carry onto the stage. For him, the differences in red begin to magnify and become the difference between tight, smooth, healthy skin around an eye and a fist-fight's shiner. He uses a finger to rub some of the excess red away, then wipes the digit on a tissue. When he is satisfied, he uses a brush to lift powder and lay it gently on his face to smooth over the repair work. He looks at himself straight in the mirror, then turns his head from side to side checking the repairs carefully as he runs his lines out loud as quickly as he can say them.

He rises, pushes his chair up to the table as he recites the words he already knows so well from eight weeks of memorization and weeks of rehearsals. "The words will come," he tells himself and then goes on spewing them anyway, as an homage his disciplined approach to acting. As he speaks, he removes his clothing down to his tight white briefs. He stops talking when he looks at his body in the mirror. It is an image he likes, a body he works hard to maintain, a chiseled tool essential to his trade like a mechanic's wrench or carpenter's hammer.

Rising on the tips of his toes, he reaches his arms up over his head stretching to see how close his hands can come to the ceiling, how far his heels can rise off the floor without giving way to loss of balance. Muscles in his legs, back, and arms elongate. Belly and chest tighten. When he reaches maximum exertion, he lowers his arms, allows his heels to feel the floor's coolness, feels the muscles of his body relaxing as he bends and touches the floor and allows the upper half of his body to release like an unused rubber band. When he has stretched and relaxed several times, he wipes his hands again before touching his costume and dressing as the squawky speaker delivers the message "Ten minutes to places!"

Though he had done his preparation work earlier, it is his habit to spend the last few minutes before going on the stage stretching his jaws once more, making his tongue articulate sounds, reminding himself of the essential act of theatre as communication with an audience. Brad Michaels never forgets the basics: His body, his movements, his facial expressions and his articulation of words working together to create meaning for the audience members' experience of the play; the same is true of his interactions with other actors on the stage and his part, Dave Singh, as person—not character. Person interacting with other people ... people with emotions, actions, and intentions all their own.

His mantra is to be worthy of the role. Be worthy of the other actors and all the backstage people who make the play possible. Support fellow actors and the people they play. He hears the words of his teachers, "Give your best performance in hopes that others give theirs." Brad admires the skills and professionalism of his co-stars, Kevin and Matt, and has enjoyed working with them, spending time with them.

He hadn't been surprised when he found several cards at his dressing table. Actors often give token gifts or cards with some kind words for opening night. Brad thought of such gestures as the "obligatory niceties"; he did it him-self. Ordinarily, he reads all of the cards when he arrives at the theater, takes pleasure in the gesture and then sets them aside until after the show—no distractions during prep work. Tonight, he had read them all but one: a sealed, notecard-sized envelope. There is tension in picking it up, a discomfort about what it might or might not say as he traces the curvature of his character name scrawled in Kevin's distinctive sweep of a black pen and his overused red hashmarks around the sweeping elongated bends of the individual letters as if trying to give them motion. It is the writing Brad has seen scribbled all over the note-pad Kevin carried through the first week of rehearsal for keeping track of stage movement, director suggestions, and other miscellaneous reminders to himself. Unfortu-nately, Kevin would leave it lying about, lose it, and later enlist Brad and Matt's help looking all over the theater try-ing to find it. More than once, Brad had found it for him, remarked about the scrawl and the two-color play, jokingly calling Kevin, "Doodles."

After a moment of staring at it, trying to understand his own hesitation, Brad breaks the envelope's seal and removes an elegant, handmade, single-fold card made of three layers and shades of precisely cut Papyrus. On the front of the card are the words, "You are the art that rises above the house like the sun or stars!" When he lifts the cover, he reads:

Brad,

*It has been an honor working with you for the past
six weeks as we struggled to find the heart of this
play. You have inspired me and challenged me to
work harder than I've ever worked to get a part right.
I admire your talent, your professionalism, and your
support. Were I "Jack" and you "Dave," I would gladly
respond to your last line of dialog with "I would be
happy either place."*

Break a leg!

Kevin/Jack

He had placed his own handwritten cards in Kevin's
dressing room and placed cards at the various stations
for the director, stage manager, and crew members to
find. His card for Kevin was addressed to "Doodles." It
praised his work and expressed sentiments of respect
and appreciation for the time they had spent together rehearsing, discussing their parts and their characters' mo-
tivations, the director's observations and suggestions. And
it expressed the pleasure he took in their friendship and
his desire that it continue. It did not, however, speak of
"the last line." He put a card under Matt Connor's locked
door; it was addressed to "BillyBob Banker/BillyBob Bull/
America," the names he and Kevin had created for Matt
when they were joking during breaks. The note spoke to
Connor's ability and talent playing two very different and
difficult roles, performing magnificently, and making the
roles so frighteningly believable. He referred to Connor as

the "force" within the cast that gave Kevin and himself so much to work with and to play off of. The card ended by joking that after all of the rehearsing and drinking of liters of cold tea from the alcohol bottles, Connor fully deserved the title of "TEA-totaler Extraordinaire." It was both funny for its misspelling of teetotaler and for its double-meaning—a statement of great respect for the actor and a man in active recovery.

Matt had confided in both his co-stars that the two roles were especially difficult for him, which was why he wanted them. The role of a drunken banker constantly triggered old feelings and desires he had to fight through; playing the role of the thug came with pains that felt even more significant to him: the brutality, willful ignorance, and hatred of people different from the characters he played. As an actor, he loved the art of making two different characters, both so contrary to his own nature, come to life.

Everybody working on the production knew Matt Connor's history: he had been an up-and-coming star twenty years earlier doing theatre, playing on a television series, doing a few small parts in movies, and playing roles for commercials and industrial training videos. Early in his career cameras loved him; audiences loved him; directors loved him. However, aging didn't. By his mid-thirties, he had become puffy, red-faced, and was losing his hair. The hair he could manage with a toupee; however, he couldn't manage the alcohol and drugs that had made the other factors worse than they might have been. Over time, drink by drink, dose by dose, he lost his wife, his children, his home, himself, and all sense of purpose. His star fell from the sky and crashed, creating a crater he could not climb out of for several years. Then someone came to his aid and slowly and lovingly guided him to sobriety—someone he refused to name and referred to only as "she" in sentences of the past tense. Now, two years sober, middle-aged, too physically unattractive for most leading roles, he is back, trying to rebuild his acting career, and secretly terrified.

The director of Dave's Place had known Connor back when Matt had been a hot commodity, and he also knew that giving Matt a second chance was risky despite Matt's audition having been a stellar performance: he was perfect for the part ... but only if he could be counted upon. The director had been honest and expressed his reservations directly to Matt and Matt's agent but was finally convinced by the actor's pleadings and by the assurances by the agent that the actor would deliver and would not engage in use of drugs or alcohol for the run of the show. "I'm never going back there," he had promised. With an understudy as a backup, the director agreed to give Connor his second chance.

Because of the concern about his previous life, Matt chose not to share with anyone else, including his agent, that as soon as he got the roles he had been going to bars in his off hours to observe men drinking, to listen to the talk, to gain a sense of how men were interpreting the aftermath of the insurrection. He had gone into a variety of bars from "dives" to what were considered "upscale" places and drank tonic water, gallons of it. "Actor's research," he called it. He talked to all kinds of drinkers: from chronic drunks to occasional users, from uneducated to highly educated people, from blue collar to white collar, and from people who didn't give a damn about the country to those who were passionate and deeply concerned about where the country was headed. With a few exceptions, what he saw and heard about the acceptance of hatred, selfishness, and greed depressed him considerably, made him long to drink to escape the majority of drinkers he encountered. Though he was happy for the opportunity to get back into acting and to have two challenging parts to play, he had decided that he didn't like the "America" he was playing.

We are on a five-minute delay. Places in ten minutes!

The voice coming through the speakers is mechanical, cold—icy cold like the incessant drone of an assembly line motor.

***

Brad Michaels slides the card back into its envelope and props it up against the wall beneath the mirror. Eyes closed, he opens his mouth, uses his facial muscles to stretch as far as his mouth will open, pulls his lips back, works his jaws side to side, moves his chin in small circles. When he is done with several repetitions, he closes his mouth again, pulls his cheeks high up toward his eyes, squinches his nose, his lips stretching into a hideous smile that overexposes his teeth. The tip of his tongue touches the inside of his front teeth as he makes sounds:

da-da-da-da-dee-dee-dee-dee-ta-ta-ta-ta-tee-tee-tee – dee-
dee-dee-dee-mee-mee-mee-mee-mow-mow-mow-mow-
moo – moo-moo-moo—mwaah—mwaah—mwaah...

At the call, "two minutes to places," he reaches into his
memory bank for a quotation he can use for the final component of his ritual: a reminder to himself to say words in
full to be understood, their syllables and their sounds: the
"t," "d," "s," and "ings" of words to be heard.

"THeeeZ–are–THee–TimeZ–THaT–Try–Me
N-'S–SoulS.   THee–Sum-meR–SoLD-ieR–anD–Thee–
SuN–SHINE–Pay–TREE–oT–wiLL–iN–THiS–CRy–
SiS–SHRinK–FRoM–THee–SeR–ViS–of–THeiR–CuN–
TREE."

The call for "Places!" stops him. He takes one last look
in the mirror, picks up the card once more as if secrets
lie in the red curves around the letters, secrets for a later
time, secrets to come home to.

***

Next door, Matt Connor has been doing many of the
same kinds of preparations but with more trepidation and
an uncontrollable desire to tell the understudy to go on in
his place while he runs from the building and disappears.
The robotic sounding demand for "places" rattles him. It
is going to happen; the play is going to happen; his part in
its making is going to happen; critics are going to happen.
Trying to turn down the noises of his own insecurities, he
picks up the notes he had written to himself to deal with
his fears: "Imagine tomorrow's reviews!" He had written

them before he left home and laid them on his makeup table when he arrived. He had read the words several times, picked them up, and read them once more:

"Star still shines! Matt Connor, provides a spectacular performance in his supporting dual roles as banker and thug in Broadway's first major hit of the year, *Dave's Place*!"

"Tony Award is due for Matt Connor's outstanding performance in *Dave's Place*, one of the best plays on Broadway!"

"*Dave's Place*, a major success, one of the best plays of the year! Matt Michaels, Kevin Lane, and Matt Connor are astounding!"

Facing the mirror, he talks to the image behind the glass. "Get over yourself." He continues talking, emphatically stating to the man in the mirror that all will be fine; he knows his lines, his cues, his places; he is well-rehearsed. He tells himself he will meet the energy of the other actors, push them to do their best, and he won't let up until the final curtain.

Outside his window, the stars against the dark sky, the endless, indifferent universe.

***

At the rattling of his dressing room doorknob and the sound of the door falling away from the jamb Matt mechanically uses his knee to push the large bottom drawer of his dressing table closed.

"You ready?" Brad asks.

Matt tries to smile. "Sure am. I guess it's time to do this thing, huh?" He rises. Walks behind Brad into the hallway that leads to the stairwells on either end of the stage. They make their exchanges of "Break a leg," and "you too."

"Give me all you've got tonight, Matt! Let's rock this house!"

"You've got it," he says trying to manufacture Brad's level of enthusiasm.

Brad's energy is spilling out of him as he pats Matt on the shoulder before they go to opposite stairwells to reach their entrance points.

Though he is shaking, still feeling like he wants to run out of the building, Matt finds that strand of courage that tells him there is nothing more to do but face the full house, step onto the stage and act, respond to cues. Act! Stop thinking about another gulp of whiskey from the bottle in the drawer or another one of the benzos he bought to calm him down. He has done more than enough fighting with these beasts in his dressing room where they sunk their teeth into his flesh, clawed at his chest right up until the two-minute warning of the god-voiced speaker that sent the beasts back to their cages so that he had time to dab carefully at tears, trying not to let them overwhelm his face. He has made them more than once already, tossed many tissues into the trash can. His time for repairs has run out.

As he takes hold of the stairwell door, he is reciting his litany of reasons to be good in his role: a career to regain, an audience to please, estranged children to make proud, critics to be knocked on their asses by his performance, an opportunity to regain his self-respect. He opens the door and looks up the two-tiered concrete steps, feels his legs turning to jelly, his skin reacting like biting insects are crawling over him, his heart thumping loudly in the cavernous black of his chest, and his eyes shifting focus, left, right, up, down, up, left ... fear coming at him like bank shots in pool with players on all sides aiming for his life as he hides behind the eight ball. "Escape" comes to his mind again, but he can't move. A stagehand comes down the stairs looking for him.

"Are you okay, Mr. Connor? They've called places."

Matt focuses all his energy, and after a moment, forces a smile and responds, "I'm fine," the quiver in his own voice articulating the lie. The stagehand watches as Matt places his right hand on the rail and pulls hard to drag the recalcitrant legs slowly up the stairs to the landing at the backstage wing and its eerie blue light. The young man who has followed behind talking into his communication device is assuring the stage manager that Matt is on his way. He confides in a whisper that he is worried, but "the actor insists he is fine." At the top of the landing, the young man asks again,

"Are you sure you are all right, Sir? I smell alcohol."

Matt Connor sucks in a huge breath of air and releases it slowly far to the right of the young man standing before him.

"I'm fine," he says, his voice weak and a bit shaky. His eyes shift away from the man's face. "It's ... it's um mouthwash you smell."

"Yes, sir."

A costumer's assistant is holding the coat and scarf he will need, helps him get them on, and walks away. Matt and the young man move to the place from which Matt is to make his entrance. The track of the main curtain makes a rattle as it opens. Lights flood the stage. Brad is in motion at the bar upstage right. Unaware that he is doing it, Matt takes the arm of the stagehand, squeezes firmly on the young man's bicep, releases his hold, and pats the man on the back while repeating himself ... still sounding unsure: "I'm fine."

"Of course you are, Mr. Connor."

5

People who want to get into the booze business in Pierlight, Ohio, buy downtown space; they pay high prices for rent or ownership knowing there is money to be made in the extra-curricular activity of student brain modification through alcohol.

Dave Singh chose the location on the corners of Twelfth and Converse Streets specifically because it was not a downtown space and far enough away that it would be a long walk or at least a short drive from the student neighborhoods. It wasn't that he wouldn't have liked the income that he could garner from thirsty college students. He simply didn't want to be part of the group that took advantage of young people deeply invested in experimenting with their limits. In years past, he worked in such places, saw the ways owners cut corners to manipulate and prey upon their clientele; he also saw first-hand the problems crowds of students caused. He wanted to offer a place for the rest of the population ... quieter, calmer, more comfortable, more customer friendly.

The corner location was part of a well-maintained and clean neighborhood distinctly different from those over-packed with young people who were being gouged for places to sleep--places where the university administration couldn't control what they did, when they did whatever it was they wanted to do, or with whom they did it. For the price of freedom, they paid exorbitant prices to live in houses with mushy floors, cracked plaster, rusted kitchens and bath fixtures, broken doors, and dilapidated furniture—some of it sitting on dilapidated porches. In the worst of the worst, student renters dealt with cockroaches and ants, maybe mice or rats, and trash piled in the side yards by previous tenants. The sidewalks of the uptown bars were only slightly better.

Dave had lived that life in similar neighborhoods when he was in college: cans and bottles everywhere, cheap plastic beer cups stacked high on porch railings as part of a salute to youth. Debris everywhere. Some of the upright cups, bottles, and cans succumbed to the rhythms of the porches' rotting boards bouncing them off their perches as heavy-footed students came and went. There were also the variations of winds from breeze to storm that knocked the uprights from their fragile plinths like seeds or cigarette butts onto the grass and sidewalks. Occasionally, an angered human cast any and all debris anywhere and everywhere as an act of defiance against their perceptions of the city and its code officers trying to stifle their freedom—their joy of being young, oblivious, and damned.

***

Before buying his own building, Dave Singh had spent a few years working for various bar owners uptown and seen first-hand the excesses of the student crowd. Making more money as an owner wasn't going to remove the daily stress of breaking up fights, cleaning up vomit, and constantly trying to repair the damage wild groups of young people can do to a building and its furnishings. What was important to him was finding a different clientele and working in a place he liked to spend time in. It was that desire that caused him to take a job working in Columbus at "Solly's"—an established neighborhood bar—for the two years prior to buying and opening Dave's Place.

Before he died, old Solly Ernst doted upon his protégé, treated him like a son, taught him everything he knew about the business. Probably would have left him the business if he could have. Unfortunately, Dave eventually learned that Solly had a wife to care for and lots of debts as a result of her relentless buying habits, and the likelihood of her turning the place over to him or selling it to him at a reasonable cost would be somewhere between slim and zilch.

Working with Solly, Dave learned that non-student types—locals, workers, professionals, people in general—expect "barkeeps" (as Solly referred to himself) to be no-cost mental-health therapists whether or not the barkeeper knows anything at all about human psychology. Solly taught him to think in questions rather than answers, to listen carefully and not to lead people to answers. Solly's theory was that people needed questions that only they could answer for themselves.

"It means more to 'em when they come up with their own answers. If you tell 'em what to do, even if you know it's what they're likely to come to on their own if they've got a ounce of sense, they'll resist it. Folks don't like somebody else ownin' their thoughts. They want to own 'em for themselves. It's kind of like how people think about charity. Most don't want it even if it's just what they need. At least they don't want it until they got no choice. But give 'em little bit o' work to earn whatever your givin' 'em—an' don't call it charity, they feel different 'bout it. I don't tell people what to do or not to do. I nod a lot! I repeat back to 'em what they say, but in my own words so I don't sound like a goddamn parrot. I try to be int'rested in what they talk about, ask questions that only they can answer like 'What-taya want to happen?' or 'Whatcha think you'd like to do 'bout that?'; they'll think you're a genius. Here's the secret, Davie: you can't fake kindness. Everybody needs somebody to talk to, somebody who'll care about 'em. If you can't be real with 'em, or if you think it's your job to fix their pains and woes, better to be one of those guys who just pours the drinks and don't talk."

During the two years he worked for Solly, Dave listened to what the old man said and watched what he did for the people he served. Dave jokingly referred to him as "Bar God" out of admiration for the way he treated patrons. Solly was generosity, kindness, and caring personified. Never lost his temper. Apparently had never had a bad day in his lifetime. Looked at every person as someone who could teach him something. Never imposed his own beliefs on anyone. Just let people be who they were and accepted them for it ... unless they were becoming a danger to themselves or others. Then Solly would take charge. He had thrown patrons out for bad behavior and had a reputation for doing whatever it took to keep drunks from driving. Solly was a man to emulate—an artist in his own right.

Then Solly died. His wife wanted to sell the bar for far more than Dave could produce. After a few months of keeping the business alive to give her the space she needed to find a buyer, Dave was out of a job, and the land was sold to a company that planned to build nicely decorated, cookie-cutter apartments at high rents that no one other than wealthy people could afford.

He left, grateful for what Solly had given him—invaluable insight about interacting with other people—and he left with the feeling of being cared for, even loved like a son—a memory to carry as he pursued his dream of creating something similar to what Solly had done: a quiet place— the kind of place thoughtful and intelligent people like to come, a place where everyone is welcomed as long as they behave. But he wanted to do it in Pierlight, his home. As he planned, he imagined creating a clean well-lighted place from out of the Hemingway story—a simile of a place where people came to write or chat with one another, to ponder dreams, and escape their fears, or simply to relax after hard workdays before going to their problems at home and long nights alone in darkness. He imagined catering to people with a passion for life: writers, painters, thinkers of all kinds. He wanted to create the kind of place he would like were he an artist, a place where there are people interesting to talk to and learn from.

Every now and then, he reminded himself that he was romanticizing, dreaming ideals, and forgetting that life isn't forever like a great short story, play, or novel that he loved to read. He understood that people free of an author's control don't always do what a writer makes them do; they live their own messy and non-linear lives—lives that don't always lead to a dénouement followed by an epiphany. But maybe, he thought, just maybe, bits and pieces, bursts of experience, might get him some of the world he wanted to live in amongst people who had more to them than small talk and jokes. ... So much would depend upon the image he could engender, the place itself—its look and feel—the image he would create as owner, and, of course, the balance between people who would come through the doors actually living up to his dreams and those who wouldn't.

Of special interest to Dave Singh was that Pierlight is a small city full of professors, artists and thinkers. It is a cultural hub for the art-starved communities in surrounding small towns and villages in the county as well as several surrounding counties. It is also the county seat and is rife with lawyers, politicians, and city and county officials attuned to local and state politics. There are business owners, school and college administrators, and support staff of all kinds. It is a panoply of underserved non-student people who need a place of their own. Dave had set out to make his place one that such people would come to. From the beginning, anyone who came through the door and behaved civilly was welcomed. Most of those who returned regularly did so because they sensed in the space and in the man who controlled it that this was a refuge from the calamity of living—a place worth treating respectfully. For three years "Dave's Place" had done well. Then came Covid.

The earth paused its spinning, or so it felt. The monthly bills continued to come in on schedule, but the customers Dave needed for keeping the business alive did not. Like so many others, he began spending down the savings he had managed to put aside. And it was going fast, draining the money earned by his own frugality and the money his grandparents had left him in their wills. Month by month he watched the figures on his bank statements shrivel to a few thousand dollars. The end was coming and yet, he held onto hopes of survival. He held hope like a fly he had swept into his lightning-fast hand before it processed the speeding shadow coming over it. Things would change for the better, he told himself, if he didn't let hope fly from his grasp or he didn't kill it in a moment of anger. He told himself things couldn't get much worse ... until they did, the previous day, and the fly buzzed against the metaphorical palm trying to escape, but still he did not let it go.

Members of the House of Representatives and Senate were set to count Electoral College votes while thousands of people were rallying in support of ...

It is on the TV again. Rehash after rehash of the events that he and so many others know should not have surprised them, but did nonetheless ... breathless reporters spewing endless speculation about what a president could have or should have done but didn't do, asking guests and panelists whether or not the "riot" had been planned or had been a spontaneous happening, questioning whether or not democracy was on destruction's eve, chewing every last morsel of guesswork anyone can think of to keep viewers glued to their TV sets or cellphones through the relentless commercial breaks that bombard viewers with impressions that they need things! More and more things! Apparently, even in the midst of a disaster, there are important things to spend money upon: better smell, better clothes, better appliances, more food, better weight-loss programs, more, more, more. Clearly, even if democracy fails, there will still be a need for toilet paper, beer, cigarettes, and toasted oat cereal.

6

Act I, Scene I

[Lights up. Curtain opens. A bar in an Ohio city.]

Dave has already cleaned the bathroom fixtures, wiped down the ceramic walls, mopped the floors. The work is done, and he still has an hour before opening. There hadn't been enough business the previous day to nudge the income scale or to create a mess equal to his effort, but he likes being here. He turns on the television, picks up a clean white towel, and pushes it once again over already shiny surfaces. The TV spews the news of insurrection. Occasionally, a separate cloth receives a fresh squirt of polish to be applied to what might be a smudge on a surface. He suddenly realizes that he is rubbing polish into the face of the wood hard enough to make his knuckles hurt. He pulls his hand back as an apology for punishing the wood and his body as a symbolic attempt to end stupidity in the human race.

More than once, he thinks about turning the TV off, shutting down the incessant attempts of newscasters to find anything resembling real news to feed ravenous and frightened audiences. He can't make himself do it. Over and over, he finds himself, polishing cloth in hand, staring once again at newsroom cutaways of people smashing windows and stepping through the debris to the interior of the capitol; people outside the building chanting threats to hang the vice-president; people banging on the doors of the Senate Chambers; people taking pictures and video images of themselves or others as they sit in some politician's chair; people waving confederate flags in the Rotunda.

Half an hour or so before opening time, he takes one last swipe at the surfaces of the bar and the backbar's voluptuous face moldings and tantalizing designs as if feeling a lover's skin. He isn't in the realm of consciously attaching words to the abstracted feelings of connection to this artifact; it is more that fragments of feelings create a series of pictures in his brain: the buying, the hauling, the dissembling, the restoration. As he steps back from the bar, he sees what no one else can: the pieces that had once been separated for months, the intimacy of their naked bodies, his hands touching every inch of them inside and out over numerous days of nurturing his expectations of them before raising them from the dead. And when that day had come, when the pieces came together as a whole he alone had seen and owned their initial unveiling, their ascension. His hands, his body, his commitment, his vision, his joy are in the very fibers of its being. He is in it, and it is in him and of him as an *objet d'art*, its being is that of a child to protect from a vulgar world. He remembers his initial jealousy about sharing it with those who would be so stupid as to touch it, set a wet glass on it, leave fingerprints on it. And when the feelings rearranged themselves into conscious thought, he struggled with the notion of releasing it to the public—the purpose for which he had bought it. However, it took some time for him to accept that the bar would always serve two masters: art and utility—his engagement in its resurrection and the public's need for something to lean on as they drink.

They tried valiantly to keep the rioters at bay, danger grew to the point that ... one person killed ...

The television voice throbbed in the background, built to a crescendo, shouting, dragging Dave out of that space in his brain where the body is forgotten, where action is an image, an occasional word, a meaning that needs no explanation. He turns the volume down.

When he is satisfied that he has done all he can do to make his business appealing to the public, he looks in the mirrors of the backbar, looks at his thirty-one-year-old body, lean, muscular, handsome still. He too—his body, his skills, his voice, his being—is part of the creation, part of the ambience, and part of the impression that people will carry home with them and want to revisit ... that is, if it survives the pandemic. He runs his hands over the plentiful hair on his head; pulls and pushes his lips with a finger to check the whiteness of his teeth; places his pointer finger and thumb at the center of his mustache and pulls in opposite directions to smooth any hairs that might be rebelling against his sense of personal care for the image he is making.

He walks toward the front door, then stops several feet back from it. He turns slowly, his eyes panning the interior space, moving from the entrance door on his right toward the refinished antique walnut coat rack, over the tables and chairs—his body moving with his eyes as they shift to the bar at the opposite end of the room, then on to the beveled panes of the windows to his immediate left ... all of it—this wholeness of his own creation—carefully designed to make the space modern and welcoming without clashing with the antique bar: that magnificent coalescence of various woods and master craftsmanship from out of the past standing at the front of the room like an American flag. He feels pride for his efforts—a sense of ownership, not so much for the place or the things in it, but for the creation as an extension of his essential self. Though he willingly allows others to visit his space, enjoy it, revel in it, most of those who come cannot fully appreciate that, for him, at least for now, this is his gallery, his *Centre Pompidou* for sharing art, not solely as object but as being. Many artist types have in their talks with him labeled the creation as old-world history in a new world setting of carefully chosen wall colors, furniture, ceramic tiled floors, and LED lighting, attention carefully paid to every inch of space. They are right for as far as they have ventured. They simply haven't ventured into the space Dave has experienced. Maybe they can't. How could they? How does anyone get into someone else's innermost thoughts or being?

There is a clacking at the door behind him as the thumb latch and bolt hit the metal plate that had swallowed the bolt's tongue. Dave's body turns grudgingly to the sounds that are now being replaced with knuckle rapping on the large glass pane of the door. The spell of the previous minutes' reveries is broken irrevocably.

A wide, red-faced, middle-aged man is at the glass. He is wearing a black winter dress coat and a scarf and is leaning forward, his forehead pressing against the glass inset of the door, his right hand forming a hood over his eyes as he attempts to look into the space beyond the door.

"Not open yet," Dave yells as he points to the sign on the door right below the man's face.

"Can't you cut a guy some slack? It's cold out here. I won't be any trouble," the man shouts through the door glass.

Dave swallows the feeling of annoyance. "There is almost always trouble when someone says there isn't going to be any," he says under his breath. The desire to hold onto the little time he can have for himself is strong. Surely, the man can go someplace else for a while. But where? Not much open anywhere for any purpose. For a second, he weighs that nagging desire to return to his own thoughts against the crushing brutality of the pandemic aided by the restrictions imposed by local authorities and by the diminishing numbers in his checking account. He pulls a white cloth mask out of his pocket and puts it over his nose and mouth. He takes hold of the deadbolt lock, turns it, and opens the door for the man to enter.

The man steps beyond the doormat, talks as he pulls off his neck scarf, and starts moving deeper into the room.

"I thank you, kind sir! Won't get in your way. Say! Really nice place you've got here." Then he repeats the last phrase, emphasizing the word *really*!" He removes his coat and lays it on a table in the center of the room, then lays the scarf on top of it.

Dave feels the cold January wind throwing itself at him like a linebacker as he pushes the door closed against it and starts moving toward the customer. But the man doesn't wait for Dave to reach him.

"Just bring me a bourbon neat—best you've got— and a red ale if you've got it."

"I've got Smithwick's."

"The best!"

"You're going to have to wear a mask, my friend, when you aren't drinking," Dave says for the sake of duty to local authorities who came up with rules useless to people who are going to pull masks down or off the minute their first drink is placed in front of them and who are going to keep them off for as long as they can afford to keep something liquid on the table. "Oh, yes. Of course. Forgot. Don't think I have one on me though. Got an extra?"

The man follows Dave to the bar, staying several feet behind him waiting for the mask. Dave goes through the swing door separating the bar from the public, reaches under the counter, and pulls out a paper mask, hands it to the man, and watches him struggle to get it on over his ears and onto his face and over his mouth.

"Sorry, you have to have it over your nose too. City rules."

"I understand. Your bar is a beauty. Where on earth did you come up with this?" the man asks trying to point at the bar while pulling the mask up only slightly over the tip of his nose.

Dave lifts a bottle of Woodward Reserve Single Barrel off the shelf and shows it to the Man who nods approval. "Good choice. Classy. High end," Dave thinks to himself even as he tries to subdue his underlying annoyance with having to open early, "You let him in; it's not his fault."

The man's question hangs in the space between the asking, the interruption of the transaction and Dave's response, a response he has to think about. There is always so much about a story that can't be said, not because it isn't interesting to the teller or potentially interesting or valuable to the listener, but because most people who ask questions don't really want answers, don't want to be bothered by the risk of getting interested in somebody new— someone who might eventually expect something of them. Of course, it works in reverse as well: the teller not wanting to risk an interaction for any of the same reasons the other person doesn't want to hear it. What passes for listening is most often really waiting: the "listeners" waiting for talking to stop so they can insert their own voices, or waiting for the opportunity to politely excuse themselves for lack of interest in anything outside their own thoughts, or waiting for any kind of pause to come so they can break away and be alone to wallow in their own woes, or waiting for the moment they have done their duty to politeness so they can turn and walk quickly to their tables or booths where intimate others look forward to engaging in their shared histories and interests—those things they have beaten to death many times over, but for lack of anything else, enjoy like sadist children kicking the carcass of a dead horse.

Dave knows the basic rules of pseudo-communication, so he doesn't go into the backstory of buying the building four years earlier and installing a temporary bar until he could afford to remodel the space. He doesn't go into the research he did in his attempts to find an antique bar that inspired him, doesn't try to impress the man with the hours of online searching, the many calls to various antiques dealers, the time it took to study pictures and descriptions sent to him, the hours of driving to see up close and personal what looked good in those pictures and descriptions only to be disappointed either by the quality of workmanship applied to the wood or by the misrepresentations given him by dealers who assumed they could talk him into a sale if they could get him through the door. He doesn't share the pleasure he has taken in feeling the wood, the sensation of placing his hands on it as if plunging them into a vat of sweet-smelling aloe lotion as if it can restore his soul as well as his skin. He doesn't share the feelings of excitement he felt when cracked, age-darkened varnish and lacquer peeled away and the woodgrains came into focus as he carefully removed layers of time, grime, and human negligence, the joy he had taken in mahogany and walnut surfaces embracing lovingly crafted, contrasting panels of light oak with minimalistic designs alternating with panels made of red and white oak and cherry mixing with smaller, intricately carved and artistically placed pieces of mahogany and walnut made like recurrent themes in a music score. He doesn't share the pleasure he took in replacing two broken mirror panels on the liquor shelves with reproduction pieces he had had specially made to match the bevel of the original, nor does he share how he had the silver and paint on the backs of the remaining old mirrors removed and the glass re-silvered to look as brilliant as the mirrors had been when they were first made. Dave Singh knows the loneliness and pointlessness of conventional conversations.

To answer the man's question, Dave tells the condensed version—the acceptable version—the one that answers a question while leaving out everything that truly matters. He tells how a friend had seen the bar and backbar in an antique dealer's building in Columbus. Dave followed up with the dealer, looked at pictures she had sent and took the following Sunday to drive the seventy miles between Pierlight and Columbus.

He withholds explanation of the efforts he had made once he arrived at the antique dealer's place of business to examine the workmanship of the dust-covered wood in the dingy light of a deteriorated building whose "Antique Store" sign had lost most of its paint, or how he carefully measured and compared dimensional figures with his carefully drawn floor plan for his own space.

Breaking from his brief synopsis about the bar, he asks the man, "You want these drinks at the bar?"

"Nah. Think I'd like to sit at a table."

Dave puts the bourbon, ale, a glass and napkins on a tray as the man walks to the table he has reserved with his coat in the empty room and sits. Dave follows. He sets the bourbon glass down in front of the customer. Before Dave can set anything else from the tray onto the table, the man has already picked up and swallowed the bourbon.

"That's what I needed. Set up another when you get a second!"

Dave sets the tray on the table and pours the ale into a mug. The man takes up the ale as soon as the last drip from the bottle falls.

"What do I owe you?" the man asks.

"Seventeen dollars," Dave says, then watches the man fumble around in his pocket for his wallet, pull a wad of money from it and lay both the wallet and the wad on the table. Hundreds of dollars.

"Take what you need," the man says, "and bring me another round. Take five bucks for yourself too."

Dave thanks the man for his generosity as he lifts a twenty and a five and holds them up for him to see.

"Know anything about where it came from?" The man asks as Dave sets the empty bottle on the tray.

"The ale?"

"No. Your bar."

As he puts the bourbon glass on the tray and starts walking back toward the bar, Dave talks over his shoulder to tell the man that he had asked the dealer for any history she might know about the pieces. She had said that she bought them at an estate auction "somewhere in Columbus's German Village. "Somebody" had inherited a building and wanted it emptied.

The man sitting at the table nods his head and moves his eyes back and forth between the bar and the table. He settles for a moment on Dave's upper body, the movement of his arms as he puts the money into the cash drawer and extracts the man's three dollars change to return to him. From the small room behind the bar, he pulls out another red ale and sets it on the tray before pouring the second round of the bourbon. The man, seeing Dave preparing drinks, lifts the ale in front of him, swallows it in two long drinks.

"She wasn't too much into helping me," Dave says.

"Who?"

"The antique dealer."

"Oh, yes! Too bad. At least you got the bar."

As soon as the order is delivered, the man drinks the glass of bourbon almost as quickly as he had drunk the first one but lets the red ale sit.

"Oh! And ... uh ... another round when you get a minute ... guess I should have ordered them all at once," the man chuckles while pushing various denominations of money forward on the table.

Dave picks up the money and shows it to the man, who once again insists on Dave taking a five for himself. As he walks back to the bar, newscasters hack up words like "threat," "treason," "armed rebellion," and "coup." He feels disgust for the faces and bodies of people shown throwing themselves at the police, breaking windows, storming the building. Anger roils within him, rises through his body like water in an artesian well that bleeds on an oversaturated plain and leaving three options for the traveler coming his way: to get wet, avoid getting wet by finding a new path around the floodplain, or gaining higher ground to see the situation from a different perspective and try to find another way. He, himself, has not yet risen to that higher ground, and he, like many others, is afraid for the future.

He touches the bar, feels the presence of lives held within its wood grains, voices of those who made it and those who have used it—people long gone who have laughed over it and cried into it about love, truth, lies and the meaning of life. He imagines he can hear their lives like haunting Gregorian chants sung in a language he does not understand but understands none-the-less, instinctively without words, like hunger. At the moment, there is nothing to be done but wait.

Perhaps he wonders, as I do, about people ... wonders if other people—humans in general—hear the melodic sounds of time in their ears or feel flies buzz against their palms like a season living and dying. I watch with him the images on the TV screen of men and women storming the capitol, Americans: Rage, defiance, violence their response to their fears while they wait for a particular god or gods unknown to justify their behaviors or to save them from themselves as they complete the symbiosis of their human existence with a collective body of hate to have and to hold as bedmates and lovers. As we watch the screen, I think of parasites crawling over their hosts, biting the skin, moving through the bloodstream of America.

As he looks at the man sitting in the middle of the room, Dave guesses impotence; he suspects indifference ... hopes he is wrong ... but these are the most common denominators for many of the lonely people he has dealt with, most of the people he knows, regardless of their education, money, or social standing. Before he reaches the bar, he has already seen enough to know what he will face if he can't slow this man's race to oblivion. When he gets to the bar, he sets the tray down and places the glasses into soapy water. He looks up to observe his only customer, his moment with another member of humanity. The man is oozing out of his tailor-made suit. He has loosened his silk tie and unbuttoned his starched white shirt at the neck. The tucked-in portion of his shirt is inching up between his belly fat and his shiny black belt. His suitcoat looks more wrinkled than it had in the previous moments.

"What is it you do for a living?" Dave asks.

"Banker," the man says abruptly.

"You like it?"

"Nope. Hate it."

"Why is that?"

"What difference does it make? I just hate it. How about you do the talking? I don't like talking about banking."

"Okay ... I did end up finding the guy she bought the bar from."

"What guy? What she?" the man asks.

"The guy who sold the antique dealer these pieces here. It took some work, but finally got a name and phone number from the internet and called him up. Friendly enough guy. He helped. I got some of what I was hoping for. More than I had."

"Oh, yeah? Found him on the internet, eh?"

"Sometimes you get lucky."

"That's what I've heard," the man says as he starts taking long drinks of his second red ale.

Dave has dealt with all kinds of people for a long time and knows the types: the casuals, the innocents, the lonely, the sad sacks, the comics, the hook-up bait, the blowhards, the instigators, and the downright dangerous. As best he can, he tries to "read" people by observing their actions and movement, the tones of their voices, the looks in their eyes and adapt to them to predict problems and keep things calm and controlled. He is more often right than wrong. However, despite his best efforts, some customers are unpredictable or predictably problematic ... most often those who can't stay away from the outskirts where waning sanity and insanity merge ... people, who through excessive drinking, drugging, or overindulgence in self-pity or anger or personal hurt or humiliation lose their inhibitions like clothing in a haphazard strip tease to expose their flabby bodies ... spittle spraying from their too-slow tongues and leaky lips ... crying, raging, attempting destruction of people or things. There are so many reasons to be angry and destructive.

Any bartender worth his salt knows that some people come to bars seeking overdoses of alcohol as their medication for resolving problems. Some people become the problem that someone else—usually the bartender—has to solve. The man at the table is, more than likely, one of those. "No good deed goes unpunished," Dave says to himself. It is a saying his mother used many times in his past to express her perception that he was an ungrateful child. He doesn't know why it has leapt into his consciousness, especially since he doesn't believe it to be true ... in most cases.

At approximately 2:30 a tweet was sent ... stay peaceful ... too late ...

"Tough times, huh?" Dave asks, though he knows the answer, knows the banker knows the answer, knows everyone who has the ability to reason should know it. And yet he asks it, like putting a hand on a shoulder to say without words, "I'm here. You are there. There is something better in a 'we' than an 'I' or a 'you' even if we can't articulate what that something is."

"Hate' it," the man says. "Depressing as hell."

"Want me to turn the TV off?"

"Nah. Doesn't make any difference. It's already in my head whether the TV is on or not."

"Been stressful for a long while now," Dave responds. "About the only time I can escape it is when I do a project

... find something to distract me. This bar for example. I restored it. Lot of work. But, you know, while I was doing it, I wasn't thinking much about how we seem to be tearing ourselves apart in this country."

"You did a nice job," the man says unenthusiastically. He drinks his ale, holds the mug in his hand, stares at it before looking to the bartender and what he is or isn't doing at the bar, is or isn't doing about delivering drinks.

For his part, Dave feels like a man in a full-leg cast trying to climb a ten-foot wall. Like it or not, once a customer comes through the door and buys a drink, that customer is yours like a foster child to be watched over, worried about and disciplined if necessary. The "trick" to it is that a bartender—a good one—needs to be like a good therapist assessing clients' states of mind. Trying to get a person who is determined to get drunk to stop drinking is like convincing an acrophobic to go skydiving. With some luck, maybe, when the time comes, Dave will convince the banker to call somebody—a family member, a friend, a neighbor—to pick him up. The easy decision is to cut the supply line between the bar and the man, let him get angry, and then throw him out. Dave wishes it could be that easy for him, wishes he could somehow step away from his innate sense of responsibility, ignore that the man will likely go off in search of some other place that will give him what he wants, especially when he flashes his thick wallet. But what if he doesn't go to another bar? What if he goes out into the bitter, tundra-like cold of carless, peopleless city streets, falls down and freezes to death? Worse, for all Dave knows, this guy might just climb into a car—two thousand pounds of weaponry with a drunk at the wheel—and kill himself or someone else if there is anyone out there to hit. He imagines being on a witness stand being fired upon by a clever attorney—the Fool's fool, a brother's keeper, the delinquent child's father.

U.S. Attorney says the president may be investigated ... inciting ... violence ... removal ...

"Pretty unnerving," Dave says.

"I don't want to talk about that. Got anything else to talk about ... I mean, no offense, other than the bar?"

"Sure. You into sports?"

"Not really."

"What are you into?"

"Drinking." The man's eyes are darting back and forth between his now-empty mug and the bartender.

"Anything you do other than drinking?"

"Nah."

"You live around here?"

"Not far away. Half hour's drive."

"Family?"

"Yes."

There is a long pause. Dave starts talking about some things he has read in the local papers—various city and county controversies— tries to call up details from his memory to extend what is rapidly becoming a monolog. He talks about a local boy making his mark on football ... one of Pierlight's own local stars heading for the big time!

Though Dave tries to get responses to simple questions, there is nothing coming out of the man, not even the "uh huh's" or "mmm's" of bored acknowledgement of Dave's words being produced for his benefit. The banker's communication is reduced to the movement of his eyes as they follow Dave's actions and declare his mind's anticipation of the moment the lifting of the Woodward Reserve will occur and the liquid slides into his mouth and down his throat, the flow of the honey brown liquid to his belly and brain. His right hand begins tapping on the tabletop, drumming his impatience.

Pretending he suddenly remembers the order, Dave says, "Oh. Sorry. I was supposed to be getting you another round, wasn't I? Got talking, and it just slipped my mind."

He raises the bourbon bottle in a gesture of apology. Once he gets the bourbon poured and the bottle returned to its place on the shelf, he delivers the drink, watches it fly down the man's throat to wash down whatever words, memories, or visions he is escaping, watches the last of the previous red ale chase the bourbon.

"You're going at it pretty heavily, my friend. What do you think about slowing it down a bit? I don't know if I could carry you out of here to a cab if it comes to that. What do you say?"

"I say I'm fine, young man. Just keep them coming," the man says with some authority and a measure of defensiveness.

"Are you going to be driving when you leave here?"

"No. No, I'm fine. Don't worry about me. I'm fine."

"One more bourbon. That's it for a while. We're not going to have a problem here are we?"

The man becomes sheepish. "No. No problems from me. One more time, and I'll back off. I promise, and I'm not driving. I'll let you know if I need help."

Like so many other heavy drinkers Dave has dealt with, the man probably means what he is saying—at least at the moment he says it. But there is no guarantee that the initial meaning won't change over the course of the next sixty seconds or shortly thereafter as time ticks toward the man's need for another drink. Dave picks up the money, the glass, napkins, and bottle. There is no offer of a tip.

After he delivers the drinks, Dave returns to the bar. His well-formed upper body stretches the knit fabric of his shirt as his arms fold across his chest and his lower back leans against the bar held firmly in place by the rigidity of its interlocking structures and the bolts he had used to fasten it to the floor. His eyes focus on the TV screen and the talking heads of an always "distinguished" panel of experts brought in by a news network to pontificate upon their best guesses as to what is happening to the republic and what the insurrection, riot or coup or whatever it is might portend for the days ahead.

[Lights out.]

7

Act I, Scene II

[Lights up.]

Dave checks the time on his cell phone. An hour has passed since his one and only customer arrived. As he pushes his left thumb against the black on/off button of his I-Phone, the front door opens. He turns to see whether it is his customer leaving or a new customer coming in. A young man, as best Dave can tell, is pulling a coat from his shoulders to hang on the rack. The man is masked; he has a young man's body confidence, muscularity, and healthy skin. He is casually, but neatly dressed. His eyes are shiny with a glint of mischief. His blonde head of hair appears to be designer cut.

After hanging his thick jacket on the rack, the man acknowledges Dave who is awaiting him. He moves rapidly toward the bar, sits on a high stool close to the wall and leans into the forearm he has planted on the counter's glossy surface. The swivel seat allows him to turn, look briefly around to take in the whole of the space that he has walked through too quickly to appreciate. He pauses at the sight of the man at the table, age taking its toll, his appearance rumpled, his head leaning forward as if a bit too heavy to hold up, and yet something dignified about him like a crushed Derby that once hung on a Victorian coat hook behind a heavy oak door but somehow falling and then getting accidentally stepped on.

Speaking to the bartender, the man, says facetiously, "Lot going on here tonight, I see." His cheeks are rising above his mask in what Dave interprets as a smile that accents the light-hearted voice that is speaking as if he and Dave are already good friends.

"Not much action going on anywhere that I know of. Really slow. Covid. The riot. People aren't coming out."

"It wasn't a riot. It was an attempted coup."

"That's hard for me to wrap my head around. But you're right. What can I get for you?"

"O'Doul's—green bottle—if you've got it."

"Coming up." Dave walks into the small room behind the back bar, takes the beer from a cooler, uncaps it. "You want a glass?"

"No. Bottle's fine. No sense having to wash an extra glass."

Dave places a thin cork coaster on the counter, places the beer on it and lays a cocktail napkin beside it.

"That'll be three dollars."

The stranger pulls the mask down off his face as he lifts the bottle to hold like a valuable collectible he is fearful of dropping. He appears to be approximately Dave's age. Flashing his bright white teeth behind his lips, the man jokes, "Hell, Bro! I thought your mask was about Covid. It's about robbery, Buddy. Three dollars? No discount for not dirtying a glass?"

The tone of the man's joke, his smile, good looks and friendliness connect with Dave in ways that feel comfortable and fun.

"Somebody's got to pay the rent around here! Tonight, it's you."

"I suggest you head to bankruptcy court first thing in the morning if you're counting on me to keep this place afloat."

"Yeah. Guess I'll have to up the prices on O'Douls."

"No. Don't do that. Wait until I leave, okay? I'm on a tight budget." There is a brief pause before he goes on. "Wild times, huh?"

"Yeah, I remember a time when if you had come in here wearing that mask, I would have had to pull the shotgun out from under the counter."

"Okay. Okay. I get the hint. I'm paying." The man is chuckling as he pulls the wallet out of his back pocket, pays, and pushes a dollar tip across the counter. "Is that enough to buy me some good will?"

"It'll do. Guess I won't be forced to fill you full of buckshot."

"I appreciate that," the man says as he takes a short swallow of the beer. "It's good to be near another actual human being. Sick to death of working from home, staying home, doing nothing but staring at the computer all day. I hope you don't mind me joking with you."

"Hell no, man. You made me laugh. I needed that. I'm not getting all that much interaction myself. 'Rona's' making life miserable for everybody. Hurting business, as you can see." Dave pours a cup of coffee for himself, pulls down his mask to drink. "What kind of work are you doing from home?"

"Writer. Hack, really ... work for the local paper. I've passed by here lots of times. Always thought this would be a good place to sit at a table and write—you know ... pretend I'm Hemingway at a cantina ... I'm good with the image, not so good at doing the actual writing ... at least not good at doing good writing."

"You haven't done any writing you're happy with?"

"Some. Most of it is crap. Stuff nobody would want to read."

"Maybe you need to try the cantina approach."

"I'm not much of a drinker, as you can see." He is pointing to the non-alcoholic beer. "Thought I might get tossed out of a place like this for taking up a table for several hours and drinking coffee. At any rate, I just needed to get out."

"I could charge you alcohol prices for the coffee if that helps, minimum of three cups per hour."

"Thanks, Bro! What a pal." After a brief pause, he asks, "Don't you worry about getting it—the 'Rona' as you call it? I mean you get people coming in here. You don't know what they're bringing in."

"Yeah. I think about it a lot, actually. But what am I going to do? Got bills to pay just like everybody else. I either risk getting it or going broke; can't work from home when your business is tending bar. Spend half my life disinfecting this place, the other half washing my hands. It's a pain. The people who come in here have changed too."

"How so?"

"Anger. Everybody's angry. Some of them come through the door assuming rules don't apply to them; want it to be like it was before. I get people all the time not wearing masks, and I have to tell them before they get two steps inside the door that they have to wear one when they're not drinking. You'd be surprised how many times I've been told—hope you'll excuse the language—'Go fuck yourself then!' and they leave, slamming the door behind them like I'm the one who made up the rules."

"Seems to be the mantra right now about lots of things. It's a cheap line. Sounds so threatening. Actually, pretty stupid when you think about it. I mean, try picturing how anybody might go about the task of doing that."

Laughing, Dave says he prefers not to think about it. "After a while, I just don't hear the words anymore. I'm not making the laws. I don't want to get shut down. I hear the door slamming and know I've just lost what could have been a paying customer, sometimes several people traveling in a group."

"Sounds like you might be better off without them."

"You're probably right, but right now I'm not liking the belt-tightening I'm dealing with."

"I hear that. By the way, name's Jack, Jack Ingram. I live here in the neighborhood."

Dave introduces himself, and says, "Good to have somebody to talk to ... and pay the rent."

"I'd shake your hand, Dave, but we can't even do that anymore. I miss that. Don't know why. Stupid little tradition, I guess. And now, the science guys are saying we shouldn't ever go back to it. Feel like we're expected to be like robots or something. Glad I'm not in a relationship right now. How the hell are you supposed to be close to somebody when there's a goddamn wall of taboo between you and that other person? Don't kiss, don't touch, no sex, stay six feet apart." Speaking more to himself than to Dave, he jokes, "Ooh, Baby, what a turn on!" Then, to Dave, "I mean, I get it. It just sucks."

Laughing in response, Dave allows his eyes to drift to the banker who is looking like a child relegated to a corner waiting for an adult to relent and let him get up to play. Jack turns, instinctively following Dave's eyes, takes in the banker's slumped posture, his disheveled clothing, his sagging eyelids, his fingers arrhythmically tapping on the tabletop. He thinks about commenting about the man, making a joke, but decides it is somehow cruel and pointless, particularly when he looks at Dave's eyes now fixed on the man at the table, his face that has made the shift from gaze to concern.

The language of the face! An amazing interaction between intentions of the mind and thousands of minute responses of the body altering instantaneously to adjust to the point of focus. Who hasn't seen joy, anger, love, hate, terror, fear, frustration, or guilt on the faces of others ... or in their own mirrors? One person, a thousand faces to make meaning both voluntarily and involuntarily, sometimes both at the same time. In the presence of others, a momentary face shift of one person can shift the faces and thoughts of some, most, or all of those present and observing. Wordless, immediate communication. As I sit here watching these men speak, my own face changes moment by moment, brows furling and unfurling, muscles pulling my lips together and then, releasing them to let my tongue wet them, my eyelids narrowing my range of vision to see the words as they crawl across the computer screen and then opening again at the pleasure I find in a word or phrase, my jaws pulling my teeth together—clenching and releasing at my consciousness of the act. Meaning translating into words with potential to outlive us all.

Jack has seen in Dave's eyes a backstory, a story growing claws in the silence between a bartender and a man at a table, a silence packed with questions too impolite to ask ... not that Jack has always worried about being impolite in other settings; it had sometimes been the best way to provoke someone to provide needed information for a news story. If there is to be a story here, it is not yet ready to be told. Whatever is there will wait beside the image he now has of Dave's intense blue eyes.

After the few seconds it takes for Dave to assess the well-being of the banker, his focus returns to his interaction with Jack and his assessment of him. It is not a conscious act to notice how a person looks; it is an instinctual one. Like humans everywhere encountering strangers, Dave is reacting to the new presence in his space—the instinctual taking in of "the other's" size, shape, appearance, power, potential for competition, and a thousand other unarticulated sensory cues we use to decide whether or not we will be at peace with one another, avoid one another or enter into battle with one another. And, of course, Jack is doing the same thing as he interacts with Dave. And so much depends upon the interpretations they make of one another. They are two averagely handsome young men of approximately the same age, both well-toned and trim, agile, muscular, full heads of hair, good skin, and consciously working at maintaining the pride young men take in their bodies before they will have to accept the force of gravity pulling them into middle age and finally into the wrinkled sacks of skin and bones they become if they live long enough to be called "elderly." That part of the assessment is fairly easy. It is what lies behind the eyes in the billions of neurons, apportionment of chemicals, in the training and experiences stored in the brain—as well as the ability of the human mind to speak honestly and to deceive—that is much more difficult to assess. So much of what is accomplished in relationships begins with guesswork and hope.

Dave is glad to have someone to talk to, someone who might engage, or at least serve as a distraction from the seemingly irremediable negativity of news funneling into his ears from the TV and then crawling around in his brain like fire ants on the thrashing body of Uncle Sam.

"What kind of writing are you into?" Jack asks.

"Like I said, I'm mostly a hack! Sometimes I don't think I'm any kind of a writer—a real writer! Years ago, I thought I would end up writing novels or plays or something worthwhile. A lot of what I spend my time doing is just crap really, mostly just a way to pay the bills: I work for the local paper. Obituaries, highlights of city council meetings, commissioners' meetings, things like that. As if that isn't boring enough, I now have to watch those same meetings on Zoom where half the time, the people don't know how to make computers and software work. I get an occasional feature story—a hot story like "Joe Schmoe Wins the Duck Carving Award of the Month," stuff like that. When I can't get a story over the phone or some other way, I am allowed to go out. You can guess what that's like when people are afraid to get near one another and don't want you in their space. Not my idea of anything very exciting. When I have time to write something I might care about, I'm burned out. Some days I think I'd just like to write my own obituary, write a believable fake suicide note, put it on my editor's desk, and drive off into the sunset, and let people think I died. Wish I could start over. Either become a real writer or find some other way of dealing with the thoughts and feelings that are always nagging at me."

"A fake death would certainly provide you with some time! Paying the bills might be a problem."

"Here's the other side of the delusion and what keeps me from writing that fake suicide note: Time isn't all that helpful when you have nothing to write about. Sometimes I think I have good ideas. You know, something somebody maybe could give a damn about ... though I'm not sure anybody gives a damn about anything anymore. But when I try to write those ideas down, they just don't come out like I see them or hear them in my head. I've written stories, occasional poems, and tried my hand at a play. Most of the time I look back at what I've done and think it's just crap. I mean, a few good lines or paragraphs here and there, but nothing holding it all together. Sometimes I wish I could have been satisfied being an accountant or something like that. At any rate, enough complaining. You don't need to hear it."

"No, man. Talk about what you want to talk about. By the way, I took a lot of literature classes in college. Loved them. I still read a lot. For a while, I toyed with the idea of teaching. Then I learned how much teachers make and decided I needed to do something that actually put a few bucks in my pocket. So, I thought about the things people always need and will pay for, no matter what. Came up with groceries, alcohol, cigarettes, and sex. They need literature too, but, in general, they don't believe that, and sure as hell not likely to pay much for it. I'm not interested in selling groceries, don't smoke, and, well, don't imagine I could make much selling sex. Too choosy about who I'd sell to. Chose alcohol."

"I guess, if I had it to do over, with what you've given me here as options, I'd probably have to choose groceries. And remember, Buddy, grocery stores can sell cigarettes and alcohol, so I'm hitting three of the four. I'd like to be a rich sex god, but like you, I'm too choosy. Can't picture myself selling it to somebody who grosses me out."

"I guess all I've got on you is a place and a liquor license. That counts for something."

"Wish I could have been happy as a grocer. Maybe, if I were really good at it—the writing, that is—it would be different. I'm mostly just frustrated right now. Can't even find enough ways to get around real people to feed off their stories." *[He pauses momentarily.]* You've probably had some interesting times, seen lots of drama—like you were saying about the people cussing you out when you asked them to wear masks."

"Not sure you could get much of a story out of that. I've had to learn to just let the crap slide off me and pay attention to folks I trust—people who do the best they can to keep on keeping on. In general, I like this work, giving people a chance to relax and talk. But you're right. I deal with some pretty interesting characters sometimes."

Dave's eyes move quickly toward the banker. He catches himself and returns to looking at Jack who is saying, "I'd like the part where people are just a little bit loosened up and can talk openly and honestly and laugh and joke, but I wouldn't want to do angry drunks. Grew up with that."

"I can't say I like dealing with that either. I don't have that too often. I guess when I decided to buy this place, I tried to convince myself that it would be better than the "dives" downtown or out in the boonies—a different clientele. I guess I was deluding myself with something out of a yuppie magazine or a story. You know, like "A Clean Well-Lighted Place."

"Whoa, Man. Impressive. You're into Hemingway!"

"I am. But you mentioned it earlier. It just stuck in my head."

"One of my favorites ... but, you know, it doesn't matter where you locate, how clean or well-lighted the place is, some people come through the doors and screw with your dream, sometimes people from the supposed best of neighborhoods. Kind of like life in general. It comes with the territory. Most people who come in here are great; they compensate for having to deal with fools."

"You're a romantic, Dave!"

"Sometimes. Or an idiot, depending on your point of view. I've had enough experience to have a fairly good sense of reality ... I just don't enjoy it as much as I like believing in the fairytale that people can be better than they sometimes are." His head rolls toward the TV set as his hand comes off the bar to point at the TV; a quick gesture to enhance his meaning. Sometimes, they're horrible—horrible before they've had a single drink and worse once the alcohol lights them up. Try telling some six-foot something, opinionated 300-pound gorilla who's getting obnoxious and aggressive that he's cut off. You know the type. Looks like he pulls live 12-inch-wide trees up by the roots for fun. His upper arms are bigger than my thigh, and here

I am trying to tell him that he's had enough. Got to admit, I've been scared a few times."

"Sounds like a good time for that shotgun. By the way, do you really have one back there?"

Got you scared now, don't I? My go-to is that I have a speed dial to the police station."

"Except when you're extorting rent money from the neighborhood hack. Then you threaten using the gun!"

"Hey, whatever it takes!" Seriously, I do like this work ... most of the time. I find most people really interesting. I like trying to get a sense of what other people's lives are all about. People come to bars for all kinds of reasons other than just to get drunk. The alcohol is just a prop. Sometimes they just need other people, like you said about yourself earlier, or they need a reason to talk, unload sorrows, think about the loves they've lost. Sometimes they just need to be angry about their lives or about the world. You hear it all as a bartender. I feel sometimes like I serve some purpose in their lives."

"I can see that. You seem like the kind of guy people can talk to. A philosopher maybe. A shrink. You should be the writer, Dave. So, who do you talk to when you need somebody?"

"Good question. Right now, it's you."

A TV voice breaks through the conversation between the two men, stops the easy flow of talk they are experiencing:

State Department official calls president unfit for office.

Speaking to the TV, Jack says, "Wow! You hear that, it's only taken four years and a coup for the State Department to determine he's unfit. Some of us knew that before he ran for office. Oops, sorry, Dave. Are you ... were you ... a fan?"

"Nope! I'm with you. We're on the same wavelength." He goes to the TV and changes the channel to ESPN and turns the volume down. "I can't take any more of it. As my friend over there at the table said earlier, it's depressing as hell."

Jack looks at Dave's face, the loss of sparkle that had been there only seconds prior, and says, "Sometimes I feel like we're living in a shitty script for 'The Twilight Zone,' one not good enough to be aired."

"I've got news for you, Bud. You are! We all are. And it's not a script."

"I was hoping you'd tell me I'm going to wake up and find it's not real. What's happening is bad enough, but why it's happening is just bizarre to me. It's like a third of the country has had the rational parts of their brains eaten by aliens."

"Don't write that story, Jack."

"Unfortunately, that one would probably sell! I've got a theory about how we got to the nuttiness we're in if you want to hear it."

"Fire away!"

"Tell me if I've got this right! So, a bunch of humans, smarter than I am, noticed that there were some patterns in the ways things work in this world. Some of them checked and rechecked their observations of those things and decided the evidence shows time and time again that what they were seeing was consistent no matter who did the checking. Somebody named those things *facts* and *truth*. Some of these facts have been facts for a long time, and they have guided the majority of people in dealing with their lives. Science, building on learned facts, gives us new facts all of the time. For example, let's just take disease for instance. Science has proven that certain diseases can be deadly and can be spread in different ways. Look at what's going on with this Covid thing. Over 3 million people died last year. That fact should be a pretty good indicator that the disease exists, it spreads, and more are going to die if we don't do something. Facts! Then somebody or a group of somebodies in power decide that these facts are not facts because "the facts" get in the way of something else the person or group of persons in power want to do. So, those people in power declare the facts to be "fake news." In fact—whatever that means to the anti-vaxers—under the new definition of *facts*, Covid is not a big deal and the medical community is lying about what is really going on. So, the facts are no longer facts. They're lies. Then somebody has the nerve to say to the people in power that their lies that are now "facts" are actually lies, and there are actual facts to prove it—this brings us back to the original facts that were then labeled lies that are being ignored."

Dave is laughing. Jack gives him just enough time to begin recovering before pushing onward.

"This accusation that the liars were lying causes outrage from the liars who are offended by being called liars. So, the liar or liars tell all their rich and powerful friends that they need to help spread the "facts" that have taken the place of the original "lies" which had once been labeled as facts. These friends, if they don't get on the bandwagon, are threatened with punishment for being disloyal if they aren't helping the more powerful liars evade the former lies which had been facts. The new facts need to be understood so people get it out of their heads that these new facts replace the lies that were the original facts. Obviously, the original liar or liars need the populace to believe the lies ... I mean facts. And, after all, facts are facts unless they are fake news!"

Dave tries to speak through choppy, tear-soaked laughter, "You've got to stop, man. You're killing me."

Barely able to control his own laughter, Jack says, "I guess we just don't appreciate the intelligence of the original liar who is not a liar but a genius. And then ... I've gotta stop this. Sometimes I feel like I'm going insane, you know? Maybe I'm the one whose brain has been eaten by an alien."

Dave tries to stifle his guffaws as he picks up a napkin to blow his nose and another to wipe his eyes. After a time when his voice comes back to him, he says, "You've got to love it when the liars—the original liars that is—get caught and then claim they never said what they said except they did, but it has to be put into the proper context: the one they want it to be put in even if they have to lie to put it there."

"You know, Dave. If we weren't living it, it would be kind of funny."

The banker, reacting to the dying laughter that had been coming from the men at the bar, sits up straight in his chair and raises his hand like a schoolboy hoping to catch the teacher's attention. As the laughter comes to a halt, he says, "I'm ready, Barkeep!" Another round please."

Dave nods, takes a bourbon glass from the shelf, pours the liquor and goes to the cooler in the small room behind the bar for a bottle of Smithwick's.

While he waits, the banker looks at Jack sitting at the bar and speaks a polite "hello" followed by the obligatory, "How are you?" to which Jack responds with the obligatory "fine," followed by, "if I ignore the news."

Faking a smile, the banker replies, "You got that right."

They have fulfilled the culture's expectations of them, even though the ritual of "How are you?" is downright silly. Most people don't want to know about how others are doing. The general expectation is to get a response of "fine," even when it isn't true, and if the rule is violated, the person who asks becomes visibly uncomfortable and will politely escape at the earliest possible moment. Jack liked testing the hypotheses with some of the people he met by responding to "How are you," with, "Well, since you asked, my life sucks." But he pushed the prankster thought out of his head like an embarrassing photo being stuffed in a drawer just as guests are coming through the front door.

After a phony laugh of acknowledgement, the banker says he too will be fine once his drinks arrive. There is a brief pause. The man looks at Jack again and asks, as if for the first time, how Jack is. Either he doesn't notice or is ignoring the quick side-to-side cartoon-like motion of Jack's head as he reacts to the man's apparent loss of memory.

Jack regains his smile and responds: "Like I said a minute ago, I'm fine. Physically, that is. Or were you asking Covidly or politically?"

"How about generally? Just talking, that's all."

"No problem. Not enjoying this ...." He was about to say "weather," but sees it is pointless. The man is not paying attention.

Dave has come out from behind the bar, tray in hand. The man's eyes are fixated on the drinks as he watches Dave repeating his ritual of setting drinks down and stating the amount due. Though there is more than enough money on the table, the banker starts pulling out bills that have been protruding from the open leather wallet—twenties, tens, fives and ones. He lays them on top of the bills already strewn about there. As he had done before, he commands, "Take what you need." Dave takes the right amount and recounts it in front of the man. The man pushes another five at Dave and insists he take it for a tip. As Dave is making his return from the table, the banker looks at Jack and asks again how he is doing.

"I thought we'd just covered that. I'm fine. How are you?"

"Me? I'm fine. What are you drinking there? Let me buy you one!"

"Thanks. But no. I'm not a big drinker. Not opposed to talking though."

"Why don't you come over here and join me? Bring the bartender too. Drinks on me."

Dave thanks the man but makes an excuse about needing to "take care of a few things."

"Can't buy anybody a drink around here," the man says.

Jack looks at Dave with a playful smile, turns to the banker and says, "You could make a contribution to the Dave-Singh-Pay-the-Bills-Fund if you want to spend your money."

"What's that? A donation? What you need? Fifty bucks? Here, take it! I got it here."

"No. No. He's just joking with you," Dave says. The color red has climbed up his chest, over his neck and cheeks. "There is no such thing." Turning to Jack, he says "Tell him you're joking. He thinks you're serious." Before Jack can respond, the man is speaking again, taking pleasure in being a part of the group, buying his way in.

"I'm serious. I'll donate. What you need? Fifty? A hundred bucks? Two hundred? Here take it!" The man pulls more money out of his wallet, pulls some cash out of his pants pocket, lays it on the table. Speaking directly to Jack, he says, "Come over. Sit down. Get a donation."

Jack tries to explain that he was joking about the Dave Singh fund; the man stares at him. Then Jack tries to explain that he is staying at a distance out of respect, not wanting to impose on the man's space, but the man isn't accepting it. He asks if Jack has a tape measure, says he isn't worried, but Jack is welcome to measure if he wants.

"Not something I carry around on me," Jack says as he laughs at the absurdity.

"Just move the chair six feet away so we can talk easier," the man says.

Jack looks at Dave, watches him shrug his shoulders as if to say, "It's your call, man, not mine!"

"All right. I'll come over there for a few minutes." He lifts himself off the barstool, picks up his beer and starts toward the table.

Before he gets there, the man starts struggling like a toddler trying to get out of its highchair for the first time without help and no concept of the distance between his feet or backside and the floor. When he gets to a standing position—his feet flat on the tiles—everything from his ankles up tests the concept of balance. He holds onto the back of the chair for a moment. "Let me clear this out of here," he says as he picks up his elegant, and undoubtedly expensive, Burberry coat and matching scarf and starts walking unsteadily toward the coat rack near the entrance door. When he arrives, he holds the coat by its collar and pushes it toward one of the hooks. He misses the hook, and the coat falls to the floor like a dirty ten-dollar sweatshirt into a hamper. He gives it one of those looks one might give to a dog that has not made it outside the door before having an "accident" on the carpet. He sighs; it is a performance of a sigh, overdone; and then bends over to pick up the clumsy oaf of a coat, braces himself on the shaft of the coatrack and uses it to pull himself upright again. He finally manages to make the collar catch on the coat hook and gives the coat a look of displeasure for its behavior and then haphazardly drapes the gray wool scarf partially over one shoulder of the coat and partially over the top of the rack.

Holding his arms out from his sides like an inexperienced tightrope walker and shuffling his feet forward to keep them on the ground, the man makes his way back to the table. He drops heavily into the hard seat of the chair opposite Jack. Dave has set the bourbon, the bottle of ale and a fresh beer mug before him and is beginning to pour the ale. Pointing to the money, Dave asks, "You want me to take it out of this?" After the man gives permission, he takes the money and jokes with the banker, "Did you rob that bank of yours, Buddy? That's a hell of a lot of money to leave lying about. How about you put it away?" The man doesn't laugh. A flash of something resembling anger comes out of his eyes, and then as if trying to catch that something and put it in a cage, the man fakes a laugh.

Dave and Jack watch the man clumsily stuffing the bills in his right front pants pocket. The wallet with some of its content still hanging half out in the open gets pushed into the inside pocket of his suit coat. Dave returns to his space behind the bar to pretend to be busy doing something important before pretending to be busy watching the TV—Cavaliers v. Grizzlies, men's bodies clashing furiously against one another to gain something called glory. When the money is put away, the banker sits staring at Jack as if confused, then asks as if for the first time, "So ... How are we doing tonight?"

Molten laughter boiling in Dave's belly is making its way up through his chest and into his mouth and is pushing against his teeth. He goes into the room behind the bar to let it out, wipe it off his face and regain composure. Jack too is fighting the urge to laugh out loud as he watches the man lift his glass of ale shakily.

"How are *we* doing? I can't speak for you, but, you know, at this moment, I'm beginning to wonder about my sanity. But I think I'll be all right." Trying to lead the way to another topic, he asks, "What brings you out tonight?"

"Just needed to get out. What's wrong with your sanity?"

"Just joking. You from around here?"

"Live in Willett. Just walked over here to warm myself up if you catch my drift."

"You walked from Willett? That's a hell of a walk."

"No, Man. Don't be silly."

"You toasty yet?"

"What do you mean? You a psychiatrist or something?"

"A psycho maybe, but definitely not a psychiatrist. Just talking."

The man takes a moment. Looks at Jack's face, the sparkle in the eyes, the set of the jaw and facial muscles speaking confidence and regard, a caring ... at least as far as a drunk man can discern. "You really a psycho?"

"I'd like to think I have it under control ... at least as well as anyone else. But you'll have to decide that for yourself."

The man stares at his glass of ale, looks sad as he says, "Got a son, you know."

"You've got a son? No. I didn't know. All this time we've been friends, and you didn't tell me you had a son."

"Didn't tell you about my son? Sorry. After all we did for him."

"What? You and me? Or, you mean you and somebody else?"

"My wife and me ... I."

"I don't have any kids myself. I was one once. Guess kids can be a disappointment. I know I was."

"You've got no idea," the man says as he turns his head briefly to his reflection on the window glass across the room.

"Probably not. I'm sorry for whatever you're dealing with."

"Thanks. Let's change the subject. How are you doing?"

"I'm not doing so well at the moment." Jack heard a snicker coming from the bar. "So, you're a banker, huh?"

"How did you know that?"

"Dave over there asked you if you robbed the bank you work for. It's his doing. He spilled the beans."

"Work at a bank. Manager."

"Really? You like that work?"

"Rather be a plumber. Just make sure shit runs downhill and water goes where you pipe it ... see what I've done at the end of the day, collect my pay and let the boss worry about the details."

"But then you wouldn't be around all that cash and making money work to make more money. You don't find that interesting?"

"Not all it's cracked up to be. Can't buy your way out of death, you know? You really a psycho?"

"Worse. I'm a writer."

"Sorry to hear it." The man's mouth hangs open, his lips are like limp rubber bands.

"Yeah, me too. Writing is kind of like cleaning toilets for a living."

The man leans forward and whispers, "I'll tell ya a secret, Buddy... 'bout being a banker. It's kind 'o like going to a strip club every day. It's right there at your table right 'n front a your face, teasin' hell out of ya. Ya can see it, you can smell it, but you touch it and somebody's gonna break your fingers and mash your puss!" Then the whispering was over. "Another drink? I'm buying. What's that your drinkin', Kid?"

"It's just a beer. A non-alcoholic beer."

"What 'n hells the point 'o that?"

"Told you I wasn't much of a drinker. I just like the feel of the bottle and being with real people, like you, and my new friend Dave over there!"

"I like real stuff. You a dry drunk?"

"Son of a drunk."

"Too bad." The man goes silent for a moment, his mind is far off in a drape-covered recess of his brain. And then he returns. "Did you hate your old man?"

"For a while. Then I grew up. I've tried to give up hate."

Ignoring Jack's response, the man says, "Hey! got a joke for you. You wanna hear it?"

"I guess so. Sure."

"So ... there are these three men in a bar." The man holds up a finger for each of the characters as he introduces them. "A priest, a car salesman, a banker and a lawyer." Puzzled, he looks at the four fingers. "Wait. No salesman. Let me start over. So, three guys walk into a bar: Priest, lawyer, banker. They sit down at the bar. Priest orders ... Wait. Forgot. Is it a priest? Maybe it's a Rabbi. Then a horse comes in ... Forget it. I think I'm getting a little drunk."

"Probably best to let it go for now," Jack says. "Maybe it will come back to you later." Jack turns his head toward the bar, sees Dave's head turning back toward the TV, his hand over his mouth and his head and shoulders shaking as he tries to keep laughter under control.

"Did I tell you ... I had a son?" The man's tongue is getting thicker by the moment.

"Is this the same son you were telling me about earlier?"

"Now I don't," the man says, and he starts to cry. He wipes his eyes on the sleeve of his suit coat, picks up what remains of the beer and tries to get it to bypass the emotions escaping him and blocking his throat. He coughs, shooting beer and cuss words onto the table. Tears roll down his face over the saggy-skinned corners of his lips onto his chest.

Jack stands up, walks to the man and puts his hand on the man's shoulder. "I'm sorry for your loss, man."

After a moment the man pulls a handkerchief from his pocket and wipes his face. "Thanks. I gotta use the john. You wait here. Okay?"

"No problem, pardner. You take care of business."

The man has great difficulty pushing himself up out of the chair and getting to his feet. When he conquers the standing, he has more difficulty finding a balance point. He grabs Jack's arm to steady himself; the crying is done. He looks Jack in the eye and says, "I like that! Take care of business. You're a funny guy. What's your name, friend?"

"Just call me Psycho," Jack says meaninglessly to the back of the man who has already turned and is staggering away from him. An image of his father stumbles across his memory as he stands alone in the middle of the room. In the echo of his thoughts he hears, "Our Nada, who art in Nada ...

***

Jack goes to the bar and sits on a barstool in front of Dave who has leaned forward onto the bar surface and into his forearms as he speaks to him in a quiet voice, "You seem to be doing well with your new best friend, Jack."

"I think he's about fried."

"Yeah, pretty obvious. I'm cutting him off. I hope to hell he's not going to be a problem."

As Dave finishes the line, there is a loud crash coming from the bathroom. Reacting, Jack jumps off the barstool to a standing position, but Dave has already run well ahead of him, his powerful legs set in motion like a racer at the sound of the starting gun. Jack stops half-way across the room, and yells, "Do you need help?"

"Maybe in a minute. Hang on!"

As he waits, Jack looks down at two crumpled twenty-dollar bills lying on the floor where the man had been sitting. He picks them up and lays them on the table. Within seconds, Dave is talking, his voice resonating down the long hallway that leads past the Ladies Room to the Men's Room.

"Whoa, pardner. Let's get you out of here."

Jack waits until Dave comes out of the bathroom trying to hold the man upright—the heavy upper body seeming to have lost the urge to defy gravity. Jack remembers the dead weight of his father seemingly doubling when he got to the point of drunken collapse; he sees the struggle Dave is having and moves quickly to help. Together, the two men walk—"carry" is probably more accurate—the man to the closest chair. They flank him as they talk, both working to keep the man from shifting sideways and falling off the chair.

"You sit right there now," Dave says commandingly, and then asks, "Are you hurt?" When there is no response, he shakes the man's shoulders, then lightly slaps his chest.

"Need a drink," the man mutters.

"That's the last thing you need, Buddy. Are you hurt?"

"No," the man says feebly in a whisper.

"Got anybody we can call?"

The banker is trying to let his head fall toward the table, but the men hold him up. "Hey, don't fall asleep on me. Got anybody we can call?"

Finding his voice momentarily, the man sputters, "You can call me sweetheart!"

"Okay, Sweetheart. Anybody we can call who'll come pick you up before I have to call the cops?" Dave waits, then tilts the man's head upward. The man is asleep. They gently lower his head to the table. Working together, they take one arm at a time, lifting them up, lifting the man's head again, and pulling the arms into a fold on the table to cushion his face. They push the chair closer to the table, the chair legs screeching on the ceramic floor.

"Maybe he was half looped when he came in, and I didn't catch it," Dave says. "He came through the door with a thirst like a man coming off a desert. He was drinking hard and fast. It was like all the alcohol in the world was going to disappear any minute and he wanted his life's share before it happened."

"Probably just as well he's out. Not a very good joke teller. So, what do you do now? Call the cops? If his son just died, I hate to see him end up in jail."

"I know. But I really don't need the liability issues with him being like this. Unless you have a better idea, I don't see how else we deal with him other than call the cops. God knows how long we might have to wait for them to show up. I sure as hell don't want other people to come in here and see him like this. And I don't know about you, but I don't want to stand here holding him from falling out of the chair until the cops come. I've got a back room with an old sofa in it. If you wouldn't mind giving me a hand, we can put him there until they show up."

Jack jokes about the bonding that is taking place amongst the three of them and not wanting it to end. Then, he goes on to promote the idea that if he is going to work, Dave will need to talk about a benefits package before he commits.

"The benefit is you won't have to look at him like this."

"You're a cheap boss. You know that?"

They lift the man up, hook his right arm over Dave's shoulder, his left arm over Jack's, the flesh of their arms meeting at the man's back as they drag him off to the storage room.

[Lights out.]

8

Act I, Scene III

[Lights up.]

As they come out of the storage room, Jack is telling Dave about the number of times he carried or dragged his dad off to bed after a drunk. He is telling of his mother's sobbing, his sister's sobbing, himself as a teenager weeping for his plight as the only son, the "man of the house" when his father wasn't. He goes on telling about his trying to humor his father until he crashed and then having to help his mother put him onto the bed like a pile of sweat-soaked clothes in a too-full hamper. Dave's eyes are fixed on him as he talks, something in them saying, "I'm sorry," before a short silence.

Referring to the banker, Dave says, "I suspect he'll be out for a while. Thanks for your help, man. You're good to have around."

"No problem. Took my mind off all the other crap going on ... or at least it did until I just now brought it back to mind. Wish I could just learn to shut up."

Dave goes behind the counter to get a cleaning cloth, disinfectant spray to clean the tables the banker had used for drinking and sleeping. He also picks up a tray for carrying the used glasses and bottle away from the table. As he walks toward the swing door, he glances at the TV, and turns the channel selector to some innocuous sitcom.

Jack is standing at the table where the twenties lay.

"He was dropping money out of his pockets. Forty bucks here." He shows the money to Dave, "I'm going to put this in his coat and put his coat in the back room with him so it's safe."

"Sounds good. I swear I'm going to hire you, my friend."

"You can't afford me!"

As he gets to the storage room door, Jack turns to Dave and says, "I'd probably be better at this work than I am as a writer or newspaper man." He steps through the door with the coat.

Dave is cleaning the table when Jack returns. Picking up his bottle of beer from the bar, Jack carries it to the table where he pulls a chair around to sit and watch Dave go about his work. "What do you say to us sitting over here for a while? I like a chair with a back. Can you spare some time?"

"Sure. Soon as I get this stuff taken care of. Not like I've got lots of customers storming the doors."

"What am I? The proverbial chopped liver?"

"Hell! At the rate you're drinking that beer, I'll be lucky if you spend another three bucks if you stay 'til closing.

And by the way, you're not a customer. You're an employee. Remember?"

"Hey! That's right. How soon can I have a vacation?"

"Not until you've been here for a year."

"Then, I quit!"

"Okay. Then I guess we'll just have to settle for being friends."

"Alright. But I want my paycheck first."

"You'll have to fill out the employment form."

"Never mind. I'd rather donate my time than do any paperwork."

"Sounds like we're squared away then."

"Did he do much damage to the bathroom?"

"Didn't look too bad to me. *[Sudden realization.]* Damn. Haven't called the cops yet." Dave pulls out his cell phone and presses the speed dial to the station. It takes many rings for someone to respond.

"Yes. Dave Singh here. Dave's Place on the corner of Twelfth and Converse Streets. Got a guy passed out in the back room. No. Think it's just booze. Yes. I know. But I just didn't catch that he came in already tanked, seemed normal enough. Yes. He's safe. I have no idea who he is or where he lives. Says he's a banker. Don't think he's going to want a big to-do about it if you can avoid it. How long? Really? Okay. I close at 2 a.m. So, I'd appreciate you doing the best you can. Thanks. You got my phone number showing up on your screen? That's right. Okay. Thanks." As he puts his phone in his pocket, he says to Jack, "They're spread pretty thin tonight so it might be a while. Did he look alright when you went in with the coat?"

"Snorting like a pig driving a steam engine."

"Let's hope he doesn't suck the walls in or blow them down."

There is a pause where the two men are looking into one another's eyes; both of them suddenly aware that a form of momentary connection—desire—has passed between them, the eye contact gone on longer than is usual for two strangers—men in particular. Dave breaks the spell first, his eyes shifting to the table.

"So. Here we are babysitting a drunk," Jack says, breaking the spell.

In response, Jack's eyes turn to the windows at the front of the bar. Another uncomfortable silence takes hold as the men process what has just passed between them.

"You're a good guy, Jack. I appreciate your help." Dave is seeking a way to comfort for them both. "A while back you were telling me about your being a writer. Have you published any of your stuff? I mean other than in the newspaper?"

"A few poems. Couple of short stories. That's about it."

"That's way more than most people ever do! What do you like to write about?"

"Common people, life's struggles, how we stumble through and survive in the chaos we're living, things like that ... not that I have answers to anything. I like the questions I have and keep hoping they'll lead me somewhere eventually."

"Seems like this would be a good time to be writing about stuff like that. What are the questions, Jack?"

"The usual easy stuff: What's it all about? Why are we here? Why are we so goddamn stupid as a species? Stuff like that. Stuff that pushes real writers and thinkers to the brink of insanity. Life would be so much easier if I could find enough excitement in a football game or in endless repetition of episodes of "Law & Order" or in mowing my lawn, poker on Saturday night with the guys."

"Sounds like boredom to me."

"Me too. I think people were meant to explore, play, create ...not just procreate and die ... you know ... express themselves, leave a mark that says they mean or meant something. But then, I get to thinking about that, and I ask myself 'for what purpose?' Pretty egotistical to think you're important enough to leave some of yourself behind—other than your DNA—after you're gone. I think it all comes down to being afraid of dying. Maybe that's why we dreamed up the whole thing about religions, living forever, and all that crap. Look where that got us!"

"Yeah. Don't get me started."

"I feel like art does that for me when I try to make it, and when I see it too. This place is a great example. You've created something here, Dave. A space with vibes. The way you are. I get the sense that I fit here. I love it. Your bar is a creation worth seeing. It's a thing of beauty."

As the two men talk, Dave explains the experience of getting and refinishing the bar ... all of the things he hadn't said to the banker ... hasn't said to anyone. And Jack asks question after question to bite into the hide of Dave's passion for restoring the furniture and trying to learn its history. Dave tells the story of his disappointment when the elderly woman who was the antique dealer said, "I don't have time or wherewithal to hang onto all the things people tell me about stuff." Her punch at the "no sale" button protruding from the face of the old National cash register emphasized her word, "stuff." When the heavy spring from somewhere in the back of the machine drove the cash drawer open, she deposited the check and pushed the drawer back into place with enough force to cause the nickels, dimes, and quarters inside to clunk against their kind and clack against their wood dividers. The hard sounds of their clashing spoke like the pointed barrel of a gun. The words, "No Sale" clicked back into place in the glass encasement at the top of the register as the slammed drawer said, in Dave's interpretation of it, "Now get the fuck out of here!" With a brief hint of pride, Dave tells how he persisted, as he always does when business owners act like their customers are little more than walking wallets and charge cards that buy "stuff"—in this case, pieces of craftsmanship for preservation and use—rather than as human interactions for mutual benefit. He would not allow the gut punch of her behavior to overwhelm him. Still smiling, maintaining control over his urge to blast her with words—words like "unprofessional," "hack," "cranky," and "crochety"—he deliberately spoke to the woman as though she might have been confused and simply needed assistance with devising a means for being helpful.

Deliberately shifting his voice to a low register—firm and confident like a seasoned attorney pressing a witness—Dave explains how he placed his hands on the counter of the woman's shop, leaning forward to encroach upon the woman's space, his intense blue eyes fixed on hers, and asked ever so politely, "You keep records about who you paid checks to or bought things from, right? Any chance you could check for me? I would really appreciate it. Anything at all. I'm in no hurry to leave."

The grizzled woman's face reddened as Dave's eyes pierced the armor she wore; she suddenly felt fear—not so much for herself— but for the check she had just taken. The piercing of the eyes was like fire, and she could almost smell his check burning, turning black in the drawer. The man in front of her had grown larger somehow; and though he was smiling, seemed unperturbed, patient, she felt intimidated. Whether it was Dave Singh, or some remembrance of a time in her life when she knew how to be kind, something made her feel a need to step back from the man on the other side of the counter. She grimaced and shrugged her shoulders as she turned to take a few steps to a drab green file cabinet. She pulled at a drawer and tried to paw through a hanging file bulging with pieces of paper poking out in all directions. After a minute or so of trying to work within the confines of the packed drawer, she pulled the file out and laid it open like a book on a severely scarred oak desk. She lifted the papers abruptly one by one, flipped them over or sideways or upside down to see what was on them. A little more than halfway down the heap that had been her filing system, she found a receipt with the name, address and telephone number of the auctioneering firm that she bought from, as well as the date of the sale. She wrote the information on a scrap of paper in a scraggly scrawl and pushed it toward Dave in a gesture that said she had done all she was willing to do no matter how long he was willing to stand there, and she'd be damned before she would return his check.

"I thanked her for her kindness and walked out the door."

"There's a story, Dave! Just the kind of thing I love. I'd have a good time trying to figure out who she was and what made her the way she was with you, what drove her to be doing work she obviously doesn't like doing. So ... what happened from there?"

"So, I called the auctioneering company, and a really nice lady there went into the records. She gave me the name of the realty company that had set up the auction. I called them and got the address for where the auction took place. Once I had that, I went to the recorder's office and got into deeds for the property, found the owner's name— the guy who owned it when the auction happened—looked him up, and called him. I learned a lot about the building and the family that owned it for several generations. Unfortunately, the nephew didn't know anything about the origination of the furniture. I've had some antique dealers tell me that it's somewhere in the vicinity of 120 years old. That's as close as I've been able to get to the history of it so far. But, who knows? Something might pop up in the future and fill in the gaps. Anyway, refinishing it gave me something to do. It was kind of a mess when I bought it, but I felt like I could see under its skin. I knew there was beauty in it still. It took a long time to get to it, but it was there."

Dave went on, at Jack's insistence, to describe the meticulous refinishing process and how it had taken him many hours spread over months because of the limited time he had to give the project. He had worked an hour here, a few hours there, a few minutes in between, when he didn't require sleep or he didn't need to be working on the books or ordering stock, paying bills, meeting with an accountant or an over-eager salesperson, or just covering the long hours required to serve customers, or dealing with myriad other responsibilities that go with running a one-person business. Fortunately, he could do the refinishing in the bar's back room where the pieces were stored and could work into the morning hours after the bar closed at 2 a.m.

He continued talking, describing the way that he had to maneuver the various pieces one at a time onto a cart, set them in place, align them, and reconnect the pieces to become two unified wholes: the bar and backbar.

When he was done, he started to apologize to Jack for dominating the conversation. Jack rejected the apology. He was thinking about the story of preservation, history, Dave's commitment to maintaining it. He couldn't help but think about how Dave's passion for the topic of history and preservation pulled him briefly out of the sense of foreboding he had felt over the recent past and the images in his head of brutality in the mainstream of America, yesterday's threat to hang a vice-president and kill the Speaker of the House, impose white supremacy; he thought about the feces spread on the walls and floor of the Rotunda. In the midst of all that ugliness there is this, this commitment to something of beauty and to history.

"You've given me a couple of stories to write ... that is, with your permission. They're really yours," Jack said.

"Take them! I'd love to see them in print sometime. But, from what little I know about you, I know you have stories in you, Jack, that don't need anything from me, probably better than anything I have to offer. You told our banker friend about giving up hate in your own life. There's a story behind that. Before you can give something up, you have to have had it. You've talked about living with an alcoholic dad and playing the role of an adult when you were still a kid. There's a story in that too."

"I think those things are all part of one thing. Probably are stories there, but I'm not sure I'm ready to write them. It's enough to boil them down to giving up hate ... or at least trying to keep it at bay ... not always successfully."

Jack pauses momentarily, reflects in a flash of time on the past, his life as a child and then as a man. "There came a point with my old man when I just got tired of hating him. When I did, I finally recognized that he was just that: an old man, a disappointed, unfulfilled, depressed old man who regretted the life he led, had no sense of how to get out of it, and just rode that disappointment right into his grave. He was hooked on the bottle. I wanted him to be the father I wanted, but he just couldn't be that, and he knew it. It took a long time for me to accept that I never had the power to change him. I couldn't save him from himself. In the end, all I could do was move on with my own life the best I could. There just came a point where I finally realized that I had to accept him as he was or give him up altogether. I accepted him ... came to enjoy his company before he died, at least his company when he was sane. I just avoided him as best I could when he wasn't. We ended up having a few good years when we could talk rather than argue."

"Must have been tough on you growing up."

"It was. Still is sometimes." He takes a moment to look at the man opposite him, see the genuine caring and interest in the eyes—eyes reminiscent of the anglicized images of Christ his own mother hung about the house pointlessly. "Hatred still slips through sometimes, comes at me, catches me unaware: things people say and do. And it's really hard for me to let go of it, step back and consciously release it."

"Same for me, Jack."

"I try really hard to think that not all those people yesterday were white supremacists or misguided Christian zealots believing they were doing god's work. I try really hard to think that maybe they're being violent because they don't know what else to do. But I keep coming back to the notion that maybe there isn't a deeper reason than I can grasp, that it's all as ugly and hateful as it seems ...

that there's genuine evil in big chunks of our population. I just don't want to believe that. I don't want to hate them."

Dave is listening, thinking that perhaps it was inevitable, the attack, this setting of boundaries ... as if we are no better than animals. In the pause between Jack's last statement and the expectation of maintaining the dialog, Dave is thinking about the animal in people that fights for the lion's share of the food, fights for breeding rights, fights for control of the cave where they can sleep safely at night with their families unconcerned with the dispossessed lying miserably in the rain and mud and shivering against the cold winds coming down out of the north country. Suddenly, the thoughts are no longer contained, "We're not animals. We have the ability to reason. We can weigh good and evil, and we can change. I don't want to believe it's all as ugly as it seems. The prez and his buddies ripped the scabs off lots of old wounds and cut some new ones, and it's going to take a lot of work to undo the damage."

The men, at a loss for answers, joke that the world is not likely to change based on anything they say about the experience of living through the previous four years.

***

Life bleeds out. Computers do not weep. Robots do not weep. Bank vaults do not weep. Most of the rich will not weep. Politicians pretend to weep and make promises for the next election of a better tomorrow into which next generations will walk in the blood-soaked streets of despair.

***

After a pause, Jack jokes that Dave's "accent" isn't an Ohio accent, says he guesses somewhere in New York. "Am I right?"

"Damn! You're good, Man," Dave says within a laugh. He had grown up in Greece, a little town not too far outside Rochester, New York.

"Parents still live there. Nothing terribly special about my life. Low, middle-class upbringing. Great mom. A dick for a father ... at least when I was growing up."

"Do you get back there much?"

"Not really. Maybe once a year or so. Long drive. Too much drama."

Jack picks up on the word "drama," but doesn't pursue it.

"I'm busy all of the time. It's pretty rare I'm not working. Had to pick up some odd jobs here and there to make ends meet during this Covid thing. Do a little carpentry, fix-up work, stuff like that. But I have to do it all around my time here in the bar six days a week until I can afford to get some help. I don't sleep much!"

"It's great you've got those skills. At least, they're marketable."

"It's like anything else: Pluses and minuses. You never know what you're getting into with some of these old houses I work in. Can't count on the notion that things were done right when the house was built or that whoever has worked on it since did things the way they should have been done. Always an adventure. I have to build the "adventure" into the pricing and still find out I can't make much off the jobs and compete with others who are just fine with taking people's money and doing yet another half-assed job. It's a curse: trying to do a good job."

"Nothing's ever easy is it? Married? Relationship?"

"Nothing happening there."

"Sorry to hear that."

"Not me. Last relationship was a disaster. You?"

"Haven't found the right one yet. I guess we're a couple of losers," Jack says, without looking at Dave's face, not seeing the sudden flicker of sadness across his eyes.

"Yeah. Well, that's the way it goes sometimes. So, what does the right one look like to you?"

Jack is uneasy. "Let's just say, I don't know anymore. I thought I'd figured it out last time around. I'm trying hard not to put limitations on the whole thing. I figure I'll know it when I see it. Sounds like this relationship thing's not a great topic for either of us."

"Sorry. Didn't mean to touch a sore spot."

"Me either. Nice deflection, by the way."

"What do you mean, deflection?"

"I'm not stupid, man. I caught you trying to flip the conversation back around to me and off of you. I've got you figured out, Mr. Dave! Well, at least, I'm working on it."

There is a short pause, both men knowing they have momentarily dodged the essential issue between them— the issue they hadn't known was an issue until this moment.

"Hey, you want to shoot some hoops?" Dave asks.

"What? You got a basketball court in the back room too?"

Jack watches as Dave gets up energetically, running full on at the bar and making a comical dodge at the last minute, stopping, making a military right turn to go behind the bar. A wide-mouthed mug, a pad of paper, and a role of masking tape quickly land on the bar as part of Dave's exaggerated motions—half teenaged boy and half happy robot. He does a silly dance as he comes out from behind the bar, picks the items up and sets them on the table where Jack is sitting and enjoying the show. This suddenly zany bartender pushes several tables aside to make a large open space on the floor and then centers the mug in the space. He tears a sheet of paper from the pad and wads it up, then tosses it to Jack. When Dave asks Jack to help him put some tape down to make a square, Jack sets the "ball" down carefully on the table as though it needs to be kept from rolling off onto the floor. Pushing the role of tape at Jack, Dave explains that his job is to hold the roll of tape and let it spin on his finger while Dave begins to make a wide tape border approximately six feet square around the mug. Together they touch the painter's blue tape strips to the floor and press them into place as Dave explains the rules of the game.

"So, here's the deal. We'll play to 10 points. One point every time you make a basket. You can't step in the box or reach over it. You can block. But you can't touch. You have to make a throw within a reasonable time. No more than a minute from the time you take possession of the ball. Shoot it or forfeit. Got it? First guy to 10 points wins. Oh, one more thing: the ball's got to stay in the mug after you throw it, or it doesn't count."

He repositions the mug, making certain it's as close to the center of the border area as possible, and then picks up the wad ball, and hands it to Jack, who says, "I've got a feeling that if either of us makes it to three, it'll be a miracle."

"All right I've got the ball first." He is suddenly in motion and trying to get to "the court" before Dave has time to respond.

Dave's reaction is fast. He is practically on top of Jack before he can take a shot. Dave's hand is in front of Jack's face, accidentally hitting him with his palm. Jack dodges to his right, tries a hook shot and misses; his ball hits the floor, takes two rolls and dies like a raw meatball.

"Foul." Jack picks up the ball, goes to a spot outside the box and tells Dave his game is flawed: "Got to have a free-throw rule."

"No fair! You're making up rules. Not in the regulation handbook."

"Well, it should be."

Jack leaps forward, dodges Dave's block, throws a straight shot and misses. At Dave's turn, Jack is blocking him and suddenly stops.

"You've got someone coming in!"

Distracted, Dave turns, releases his grip on the "ball." Jack grabs it, spins around Dave toward the mug and tries to drop it in. Dave catches him cheating and calls "Foul." After a few minutes of play, teasing and more cheating, Dave tries to make a shot and Jack goes to block him, stumbles forward and ends up wrapping his arms around Dave to keep himself from falling. Their bodies against one another, they feel the pull of desire. Instead of releasing him, Dave wraps his arms around Jack's upper torso; they look at one another for a moment, holding one to the other still unsure of how to proceed. Their arms release slowly. Jack finds his balance; he steps back and slides his hands slowly down Dave's arms before pulling them back to his own body.

"Sorry. Thanks for catching me before I landed on my face."

Speaking just above a whisper, Dave says, "It's okay, Jack. Nothing to be embarrassed about. It was nice."

"It really was an accident . . ."

Cutting Jack off, Dave says, "Don't worry about it. Like I said, it was nice."

Again, the men look at one another, trying to read what is not being said. Jack's embarrassment fades. He doesn't turn away; a hint of a smile comes into his face in the brief absence of words. Dave picks the ball up from the floor and starts to take a cheat shot at the mug. Jack blocks.

Outside the bar a man watches them through the front window. When he enters, he is scowling. Dave and Jack stop the game immediately. Dave pulls his mask into place. Jack follows suit. A summer ball cap—"Cincinnati Reds"—sits on the man's head with the brim tilted slightly to the left side. He is wearing an unzipped orange hunter's vest lined with camouflage green over a tee shirt that is too tight over his middle-aged, well-fed belly that hangs over his jeans like too much leavened bread dough in a pan. The over-sized silver buckle of his belt shows a diesel truck racing out of the design and heading straight-on toward the person looking at it. His high-top work boots are snow covered. Before speaking, he stamps his feet on the mat inside the door without breaking his stare at the younger men, one of whom is watching the cinder-embedded snow falling onto the floormat; the other of whom is fighting the stereotypes that are flooding his brain.

"What the hell kinda bar is this?" The man's dark eyes move warily back and forth between Jack and Dave.

Jack smiles as he glances at Dave and then goes to the "court" to pick up the "basket" and "ball." Dave welcomes the man.

"Just having a silly game. You know how it is with Covid and all. Just filling some time." Finding his authoritative, yet friendly voice, he adds, "Sir, I have to ask you to put on a face mask while you're in here."

Immediately angry, the man speaks loudly, "Are you serious? In a bar? You're seriously wantin' me to wear a fuckin' mask?"

"I don't make the rules. It's city-wide. You have to wear the mask when you aren't putting a drink in your mouth."

"I didn't see a mask on your face until I came in. So, lets us just pretend I'm going to be playin' a game or drinkin' the whole time I'm here."

"You're right. I should have been wearing it. I'm lucky I didn't get caught. But, look. You don't have to like it. I've got no choice. If an inspector comes in here, right now, I could be shut down and there won't be any drinks for anybody. You're not drinking right this minute, so put a mask on or I can't serve you."

"JE-SUS H. CHRIST! Gimme a fuckin' mask and gimme a goddamn drink."

Dave pulls out a fresh mask from behind the bar and hands it to the man who pulls it forcefully out of Dave's hand and puts the elastic straps behind his ears and pulls it up over his mouth.

"Sir, it has to cover your nose as well as your mouth." Dave turns to Jack and asks him to pull the tape from the floor."

"Sure thing, Boss." Conveying a smile through upraised cheeks, Jack looks at Dave, rolls his eyes, and nods toward the customer. Dave returns the gesture as he watches the man grudgingly pulling the mask up over his nose.

"You satisfied now? Any grown-ups around here or just you two boys?"

"How about we start over? I'm just trying not to get shut down. What can I get for you, Sir?"

"Gimme a bottle o' Bud, an' turn up the TV."

When Dave puts the uncapped beer bottle in front of the man, he says, "That'll be three dollars."

The man pulls his mask off and throws it on the counter. "I guess that explains why this place is empty."

Ignoring the criticism, Dave takes the five-dollar-bill the man has tossed on the bar and returns the change, which the man grabs greedily and stuffs into his front pants pocket. Dave walks out from behind the bar, goes to the table where Jack is sitting. He pretends not to hear the man at the bar when he says, "Candy-assed little prick!"

The "basketball" irretrievably enmeshed in the sticky mass of wadded tape, sits alongside the tape roll, pad, and mug. Jack has pulled down his mask again to nurse what is left of his original beer after moving tables and chairs into their positions. He has listened to the exchange between the men at the bar, kept an eye on Dave, readied himself to defend if necessary. As Dave makes his way toward the table, his eyes are fixed on the wad of tape and paper and items to be put away. He doesn't speak, just picks up the collection of materials and carries them past the man at the bar and tosses the wad of paper and tape into the trashcan behind the bar and places the other items on a shelf under the counter.

An innocuous sitcom is on the television screen.

"Hey! Turn the channel to Fox! I don't wanna watch this bullshit," the man's voice grates on the air between himself and the bartender.

"I can turn it on sports, or I can turn it off. Which do you want?"

"Another reason why you got no customers in this shithole."

"Buddy, you are more than welcomed to go elsewhere if you don't like it here."

"Just turn it to ESPN unless its sissy-assed golf or queer-boy figure skating."

"Mister, I don't want any trouble with you. But if you keep talking like that, you're going to have to leave."

The man gets up off the stool and squares himself to Dave. "What's your deal, Boy? You and your buddy over there can't handle a little man talk?"

"Yeah! We can handle man-talk, but man-talk doesn't have to be like what you're saying. Why don't you just sit there and finish your drink. We'll see what's on ESPN." When he sees that the basketball game is still underway, he feels a sense of relief. He turns the volume up as the man leans back on his stool and mutters a litany of barely audible cuss words.

Walking past the man staring at the TV, Dave closes his eyes, squeezes his forehead between thumb and fingers to rub away the hostility he is feeling before reopening his eyes to see where he is going. Jack waits, knowing there are moments when it is best not to speak, moments when one man knows that another is on the verge of losing his temper and needs not be helped, needs not to be cajoled, needs not to be reasoned with, needs to be left alone. He watches Dave pick up a bottle of hand sanitizer and pump some gel into his hand, then rub his hands together furiously, driving the gel between the fingers and up onto the wrists while the man at the bar looks at him with disgust.

When he gets back to the table and sits, Jack knows the moment of danger has passed. Speaking in near whisper, "Real piece of work—this guy—huh?"

"He's trouble. Makes me real uncomfortable." "Seems like he could explode pretty easily."

"That's my read of it. Look. You don't have to stay if it starts getting to you. I've spent a lot of my life working alone in here and dealing with all types, including people like him."

"You think I'd leave you alone in here with him? Might come back and find you dead. I've got your back. I'm on the payroll. Remember?"

Picking up on Jack's attempt to help him destress, Dave says, "I appreciate it. Think he could probably take both of us though." Recognizing that whispering often provokes bullies, he speaks louder, "And anyway, you quit."

Matching the volume, and laughing, Jack asserts, "So, I un-quit!" Then he lowers his voice again to conspiratorial level, "He sure as hell doesn't seem to like being here, so maybe he'll finish his drink and leave. Right, Boy?

The man turns abruptly to face Dave and Jack. He yells, startling them, "Hey, Barkeep! Give me a shot of Jack!" He turns back to the TV. Jack covers his mouth, hunches his shoulders, pretends to be shaking in a state of panic—a performance for Dave's benefit.

Dave chuckles, makes an aside to Jack as he arises, "Shit! So much for that theory. Relax, Jack. He doesn't know your name. He means Jack Daniels."

"I knew that, Dave," he says as he makes a gesture of punching Dave's arm.

When Dave has set the shot in front of the man, he tells him the cost. The man complains about the price again, makes a statement that Dave is gouging him, pulls out money and pays grudgingly. As he takes the money, Jack looks straight into the man's eyes and asks, "Can I ask you a question?"

The man looks past Dave to the TV. "What?"

"So far, you've made it clear you don't like me, you don't like the rules, you don't like the place, you don't like the prices, you don't like what's on TV. Why are you staying here? There are other bars in town."

The man turns from the TV. His eyes narrow beneath his heavy brows. He picks up the shot, drinks it all at once, wipes his lips on the back of his hand, leans forward to glare at Dave. "What? Did I hurt your feelings? What are you? A little girl?"

"I'm the owner of this place. And I don't understand why you are here if you hate it so much."

"Maybe I wanted to see where the eggheads and fags like you and your buddy over there hang out. Why I'm here is none of your goddamn business."

"Okay, I think that's about enough. If you're going to be abusive, you're going to have to leave."

"Yeah? 'Abusive'? Ain't you the gentleman! Now who's going to make me? You? Ain't nothin' abusive 'bout callin' a spade a spade."

"I'd love to educate you about what you just said, but I have a feeling it would be a waste of time. You need to leave. If I have to call the cops, I will."

Mocking Dave, he says, "Oooh! I'm shakin' in my boots. An' you ain't edicatin' me about shit!"

"You got that right." Dave pulls out his cell phone, hits the speed dial, and waits until someone from the station answers. "Dave Singh again. Dave's Place on the corner of Twelfth and Converse Streets. Got a customer who is being verbally abusive. No, another guy. No. Completely different situation. He won't leave. I'd like him removed. Can you get somebody over here right away please? Okay. Thanks." He presses the disconnect button and puts the phone back in his pocket, looks over at Jack, then faces the man.

"I've called the police. They'll be here shortly."

"No shit! I was sittin' right here list'nin', you little chicken-shit, pantywaist. I oughta snap you like a pretzel."

Jack has risen from the table and comes rapidly to the bar. He squares himself to the man, speaks in a strong, low voice, his eyes intensely watching to see how the man is going to react.

"Mister, you're not snapping anybody like a pretzel or a stick or anything else. I don't know what your problem is, but there's no need for the way you've been and no need to let this whole thing get out of control. Why don't you just head on out the door and spare us all a lot of grief?"

"You think I'm scared because there are two of you scrawny-assed pussies in front of me? I'll go when I'm ready."

"What's it going to take to get you out of here? Jack asks, trying to maintain a look of self-confidence.

Now there's a intrestin' question! How about this? How about you admitting you are pansy-assed little queers.

Dave, indignant, says, "I'm not even responding to that . . ."

Jack pulls off his mask, cuts Dave off, and says, "OK, I'll admit it: I'm a pansy-assed little queer; so, now you can leave."

"You fuckin' disgust me."

"You know, my parents said the same thing. Yup! That's me: disgusting. You got what you wanted. Now leave."

Dave's voice is loud, "Jack, you don't have to give in to this guy."

Still staring at the man, Jack says, "So, you hate me ... us ... obviously. We make it more difficult for good people like you to get what you got coming to you."

"You perverts and others like you've fucked up everything good in this country."

"Yeah. I'm really sorry about that. Tell you what. After you leave, I'll go kill myself."

"Seeing that Jack isn't going to back away from what is likely to become a fist fight, Dave says, "Come on, Jack. You're not going to change him."

The man stands up, puffs his chest, says, "I ain't changing shit for the likes of you."

Racing into the words of war, Jack—scrappy like a bantam rooster—is talking to Dave but staring into the man's red and angry face.

"I'm not trying to change him. Just having a friendly little chat with the man."

Now, he talks directly to the face beneath the ball cap: "Right, man? Like you said, "Can't change shit." We're getting to be friends here; we know shit about each other."

"Goddamn right! We know Jack Shit about each other, and you keep mouthing off, I might just start feeling like I want to knock you on your ass. Probably kill you if I punch your fag face."

"I appreciate you not punching me, mister. I'd hardly be much fun for a guy like you. Come on, I was really enjoying getting to know you. I think we're going to be good friends."

"You're a fucking asshole, you know that?"

"Yeah, I know it. I'm an asshole. I'm a loser. I only wish I could be more like you so I could straighten out my miserable life."

"I'm sick of lookin' at you. Get out of my face."

Dave trying to deescalate the situation, says loudly, "The cops are on their way. Why don't you just leave before this goes any farther."

Reminded of the police being on their way, the man pushes Jack, causing him to take a few steps back while trying to maintain his balance. Speaking to Dave, he says, "Ya know what? Neither one of ya is worth me gettin' blood on my knuckles and sittin' in jail for." He walks toward the door, but when he gets close to the table where the men had been sitting, he uses his forearm to sweep Jack's beer bottle off into the air to crash against the side wall and fall to shards as it hits the floor. He grabs a chair and throws it on its side, and then another on top of it before going out the door and leaving it swinging in his wake. Dave walks to the door and closes it against the cold coming at him like the truck out of the man's buckle.

"Well, that went well, don't you think?" Jack is smiling when he throws the line at Dave like one of his game balls.

"Let's just say that's debatable. What in the hell was that all about?"

Jack is picking up broken glass and then takes a look at the damage to the wall where the glass had hit it. Dave is righting chairs and returning them to their places. There is a tension between them.

"All what?"

"You!"

"I was just trying to keep you from getting your teeth punched out. I just reacted. I think there's a story in it. You know, a bully comes into a bar and does his best to rile somebody up enough to want to swing at him so that he—the bully—is justified in beating the crap out of the guy who got riled up. So instead of letting the innocent bartender, who the bully thinks deserves a beating, get beaten, some nobody distracts the desperado and admits he's everything the bully says he wants to beat up. But the new potential beatee takes the fun out of it for the beater and, hopefully, the police show up before either of the potential beatees are beaten. Of course, the hero of the story is secretly hoping the bully isn't actually going to execute him or something like that."

"But you didn't know! He could have killed you. You agitated the crap out of him." Irritated, he goes to the bar to get a cloth and disinfectant. The two men continue to talk as Dave cleans the bar area where the man was, then walks back into the room, sets the cleaning supplies on a table, and starts wiping every surface the man touched. Then he puts the cloth and disinfectant away before going to the back room and bringing out a broom, dustpan and waste basket. He picks up the hand sanitizer from behind the bar and sets it on the table ... all of this activity while Jack objects to Dave's being upset.

"Could have killed you too! I figured you were worth the risk. Most bullies are really cowards at heart. When I'm nervous, I talk a lot. Just spit out whatever's in my head ... Maybe I could have toned it down a bit."

"A bit? How about a lot?" Dave's voice is concerned, but not angry.

"Okay. I could have done better. But it all worked out in the end." He pauses for a moment as it dawns on him that he is wearing a school-boy-I'll-pretend-to-be sorry,-but-I'm-not-grin. As he thinks about it, he realizes he has probably been carrying his cocked lips, his puffed chest, his eye-gleam manifestations of pride like an award for masculinity ever since the bully walked out the door. His hand comes up to his mouth, passes over his lips to push them back into something resembling what they had been before the encounter. When his hand falls from his face, he looks at Dave and asks when the police will be arriving.

"All they would say was that they would try to find some-body to send, but they are so short-staffed they can't be sure how soon they might get somebody out. I just hoped the call might scare him and make him want to leave."

The tension between them has gone.

"Well, it probably had some kind of an effect on him. I mean, he did leave."

When the broken glass has been swept up, Jack returns to his previous place at the table and sits down.

"You want a replacement on that O'Doul's?" Dave asks.

"Sure! Let's get wild and crazy."

They continue to talk while Dave is in motion retrieving, opening and delivering two bottles: one for himself and one for Jack.

"Sometimes I wonder how I landed on the same planet with people like that. Where in hell does all that hate come from?"

"If I could answer that one, I'd probably be doing something that pays more than being a newspaper man in Podunk, Ohio."

Dave sets the beers on the table, pushes one at Jack. Jack takes a drink while Dave goes quickly to the storage room and checks in on the banker before sitting down. "For whatever it's worth, our other friend is still snoring away in there. Don't know what we'll do if the cops don't take him."

"We'll work something out. If nothing else, you can take him home with you." After a brief pause, he says, "You know, if you're okay with it, we could get his wallet. Might find something there so we have somebody to call."

"Hate to go feeling around in some drunk guy's pants."

"I doubt he's going to know it one way or the other. Anyway, he stuffed it in his jacket pocket You want me to do it?"

"Probably best you let me do it in case he wakes up and starts blaming somebody for stealing it. And, by the way, if he's going home with one of us, it's not going to be me. So, you better hope the cops come or you might be snuggling up with him.

"No way! Not me. He's not my type. He's your problem, Buddy."

"Let's give it some time. It's only nine o'clock."

Jack mentions he owes for the beer and reaches for his wallet, but Dave stops him.

"Hell, no. This one's on the house. Least I can do. By the way, I really appreciated you coming over to help me out when that guy started getting in my face. 'Right friend-ly of ya, Pardner.' Dumb. But friendly.

"No problem. We're sidekicks! Remember? Must be. You just bought me a beer."

"Don't get too used to it, Bucko!"

"Bucko! Really? You called me "Bucko?" What century are you in, Bro?"

"Sorry! Have no idea where that came from. Maybe my grandfather said it when I was a kid."

"Bucko!' I love it."

"Funny how things like that pop into your head."

"Yeah. Speaking of which, can I ask you something, Dave?"

"Sure?"

"We had a moment back there while playing that dumb basketball game ...."

[Cutting him off.] "Whoa, Buddy. It wasn't dumb. I'm going to market it."

"Okay. Sorry. That PHENOMENAL basketball game! We had a moment. You said it was nice. You weren't turned off by it?"

"Jack, I said I liked it. I'm okay with it, with you."

"I'm not sure what to say."

"Why do you have to say anything?"

"I'm a writer. Always have to say something in one form or another. You heard me with that guy. I can't shut up sometimes."

"How about we just say we enjoyed it? How about we just say we're sitting here together enjoying one another's company and let it go wherever it goes?"

"I like how I'm feeling right now. I like being with you."

"Me too, Jack."

"I guess I kind of got the impression you weren't looking for anybody. I assumed you meant with a woman."

"You know what they say about assuming? Right now, I just want to enjoy this moment. Can we do that?"

"I'm enjoying the hell out of it. Drunks and bigots aside, that is."

"We've had a night so far, haven't we? And it's still early."

"I've got to say it's been interesting."

"That's an understatement!" Dave's mind drifts for a moment, and then he comes back into the present. "I was just thinking about the last guy I was with. I thought I had found the one. I haven't been with anyone since then. A long time. Turns out the only person he really loved was himself. Everything was great as long as I catered to his needs, as long as I didn't need a life of my own. It was like I was in a ménage à trois where I loved him, he said he loved me, but he was also in love with himself: If he had been an artist, he would have painted himself as the naked Narcissus loving his own reflection on the water. We talked about him. We dreamed futures for him, and when I'd remind him that I'm a person too, he acted like I was trying to steal something from him. Sometimes he was able to get outside himself to consider my needs. He bought me things, took me out to nice places to eat once in a while, went on a couple of short trips to places I wanted to go when I could break away from here, but somehow it always felt like he did those things to earn more attention for him than for showing love for me. His gifts felt like pay-offs rather than love."

"I'm sorry you didn't get the love you deserved, that everybody deserves."

"My own fault, I guess. I started out blind to who he really was, and then I hoped he'd change. I gave him everything I had, and it still wasn't enough. Felt like I was dying sometimes. He even hated me having this place. Expected me to be available any time he wanted me to be so that I could be doing something he wanted to do."

"Nobody should have to give up everything he is for someone else. That's not a relationship, that's ownership."

"Well said, Shakespeare. But you know what? I genuinely loved him, wanted him to be happy, wanted him to have the best that I could give him. I guess I just hoped that he'd want the same for me. And when I finally figured out it was always going to be his way, I had to look honestly at myself and recognize that I was going to die in the relationship. The essential me was going to die. One day, I just loaded up my car with all my stuff, waited for him to come home and told him I was done. Then I walked out the door with him yelling at me that I was a selfish son-of-a-bitch, a deserter. Absurd, *him* calling *me* that. I think this is the first time I've ever told anybody about it. Other people knew we split, but no one knew why, at least how it happened from my perspective."

Putting his hand on Dave's arm, Jack says, "I'm glad you had the guts to save yourself. We shouldn't have to make choices between existing to serve someone else's ego and losing ourselves."

As Dave raises his free hand to place it on top of Jack's and they lean toward each other ... a crash from the back room causes them both to leap up.

"What now?" Dave shouts as he is running to the storage room. Before Jack can catch up, Dave is talking loudly, authoritatively and rapidly as Jack looks in and turns his head away from the image of the banker's penis hanging out of his pants. "What are you doing, man?" Jack states more than asks. "You can't do that here. Come on. Zip it up. I'll take you to the bathroom."

Now standing outside the storage room, Jack waits for Dave and the banker to come to him. When they arrive at the doorway, Jack takes his place helping to hold the man up.

"Thanks, Jack. Got to get him to the toilet. He was trying to pee in the waste basket."

"I got the full, frontal view when I got through the door. Not a sight I want emblazoned in my memories."

When they get him to the restroom door, Dave says, "I'm going to have to go in with him and help him out, get him to sit down. Space is too small for both of us, but I might need your help when he's done."

"No problem, Boss." He releases the man to Dave at the doorway, comes back into the room. On a whim—perhaps as reaction to those moments of pleasure, the thoughts and feelings that had risen up through him like dream before the banker intervened—he goes behind the bar to get the large-mouthed mug and paper: something to burn the energy bubbling in his brain. As he bends over to get them from a shelf, he sees the shotgun hanging from two large C-shaped brackets—exaggerated cupholders; cupholders on steroids—attached to the underside of the bar making the gun accessible without interfering with the various glasses and bar supplies on the shelves. The walnut stock is smooth and clean, the barrel heavy in Jack's hand as he lifts it off the hooks, feels the seriousness of it like a scalpel in a surgeon's hands, imagines the carnage of it when it speaks. And now he knows it is there. It is real. Dave had not been joking. Solemnly, he returns it to its hangers like handling a gold candelabra from a sacred ritual. When the gun is settled, he removes sheets of paper from the pad of yellow, lined paper and makes four "basketballs." As Dave had done earlier, he carries the "game pieces" out into the room, pushes several tables aside, and places the mug in the middle of the open space. Hook shots, straight shots, fake jump shots ... he tries them all. He even tries bouncing the balls into the cup. No baskets. After a few more shots, he hears the clunk of the bodies banging on the door and wall of the bathroom as Dave tries to hold the man up and get him into the hallway.

Even between the two of them, the banker is barely able to stay upright. His head falls forward pressing his chin against his chest, his face drained of all but the dregs of consciousness, the fundamental component of humanity: the ability to transfer and receive signs and symbols.

"I couldn't get him to tell me anything about who he is, his name, who I can call, where he lives ..."

The banker, as if trying to rise up out of his stupor, mumbles something unintelligible and then makes some sound Dave interprets as "house." Hoping that this is the moment when he can finally put the pieces together, Dave says, "House? What house? What street? What's your name?" The man doesn't respond.

"Can I look in your wallet?" Again, there is no answer. Dave reaches into the jacket pocket for the wallet, flips it open. Limited to one hand, he tries to look into the spaces that ordinarily hold credit cards, pictures, licenses, and finds nothing. "All kinds of cash and lots of nothing else. No ID of any kind." The man mutters what sounds like, "sto-mony."

Taking his best guess as to the meaning, Dave says, "Nobody stole your money. I just put your wallet in your coat."

Man lifts his red, bloodshot eyes briefly toward Jack and says, "nah-done."

What are we talking about here, Buddy?"

Barely at the level of a whisper, the Banker makes an indecipherable sound.

Can you tell us your name?"

"Nope." The word comes out succinctly and loud enough to be heard outside on the street.

[Lights Out.]

9

Act I, Scene IV

[Lights up. Dave and Jack are sitting at a table talking.]

"I don't know his work very well," Jack says. "I kind of lost heart when Stewart left the show. I haven't tuned in since then. He was a genius. I wish I had his talent for getting through all of the bullshit politicians throw at us. I mean, why can't we have more of that? Hilarious, but also serious as hell. Great political commentary. I really miss him."

"Oliver has a way of cutting right down to the bone just like Stewart did! He just does it with a British accent, which I find hilarious."

"I probably haven't given him a fair shake. I've really only picked him up a couple of times on the internet. Truth of the matter is, I kind of dismissed him. You know ... a Brit getting at the underbelly of this country. But then, why not? He might have a better view of it than we do. I haven't really given him a chance."

"Give him another look, Jack. I have a feeling you could really learn to like him; he's a smart-ass like you are." Dave pauses, looks at his cell phone for the time. "Ten o'clock. Better go check on our guest room and see how our in-house banker's doing. Be right back."

"You might want to knock first in case he's naked or something."

Dave opens the door to the back room and turns on the light. Jack has the opening mouth of his beer bottle up to his lips when he hears Dave yelling from the back room.

"What the hell? What the goddamned hell?"

They are not just question words, they are confusion, frustration, fear ... all in one. Getting up, Jack is imagining the so-called guest has pulled another stunt, maybe peed on the floor again, or broken something, or fell off the sofa, or was running around naked and wedged his head under a chair, done something foolish Jack hadn't imagined. Given what he has seen so far, nothing the man has done is going to surprise him. Before he gets to the door, he asks with a hint of a laugh and in a loud voice, "What's he done *now*?"

Dave comes out to meet him like a father of a teenager who has run away from home, the father's eyes fearful and filled with guilt, "He's gone!"

Not expecting the answer he has received, his voice becomes one of concern. "What do you mean, he's gone?"

"He's gone! Him, his coat, everything. Must have gone out the rear door."

"Shit. He'll die out there in the cold."

"I can't leave the bar. Can you go out and see if he's anywhere in sight? I'll call the cops."

Jack takes a step to the side to get around Dave and go into the storage room, but Dave grabs his arm, holds it firmly, kindly. "Put your coat on, Bucko. It's cold out there. I don't want to lose you too." Jack walks quickly, determinedly to the coat rack, grabs his coat, puts it on, rushes past Dave into the storage room and out the metal door, flinging it on its hinges against the doorframe and swings back against the latch that makes a hard metallic clunk as it catches.

Dave pulls out his cell phone, hits the speed dial as he makes his way to the bar. It takes six rings before someone answers.

"Dave Singh here again. Dave's Place on the corner of Twelfth and Converse Streets. I know, I know. You're swamped. Got a new situation here. Remember I told you about the drunk guy we had in the backroom? He's gone. No, I'm not cancelling the call. I mean, I'm cancelling the first call, but this guy is very drunk and he's out in the cold. I don't know where he went or how he went. He slipped out the back door. I've got another guy out looking around the building for him, but he could have gone anywhere. No. Not the guy looking for the guy but the guy himself. I don't know what I expect you to do! I know you're swamped. You've made that clear. Are you going to do anything? No. That guy left too. No, he wasn't drunk. He was just verbally abusive. Of course, I told him to leave. But he said he wasn't going to. And then he did. I didn't call you to tell you he left because I still expected you to come for the first guy. I was going to tell you then that I didn't need you for the second guy. No, I don't see this as wasting your time. Can you please try to find somebody who can look for the man who left? No, the first man, the drunk man. I don't know where you should look. I'm not a cop! Where do cops look when a person needs to be found? Listen, I would really appreciate your at least driving around the local streets to see if he's walking around or if he's laying in a heap some-where. He looks like he's drunk as hell; that's how you'll recognize him. Thank you!" After he turns his cell phone off, he looks upward into the earless space of the empty room. He thinks of screaming. He imagines the person who took his call reaching for a peanut butter sandwich and throwing the note—assuming a note was written—into the nearest trashcan atop ten to fifteen Twinkies wrappers.

"You're not going to do a goddamn thing!" He shouts at the phone as if it is responsible for his frustration with the police department. The words reverberate from the walls, like most words thrown out at the world, to fall and die on the floor for lack of people listening.

As he tries to get his frustration under control, the front door opens noisily behind him as it hits the doorstop. Reacting to the bang and the clunks of the door trying to settle itself, he turns around to see Jack being pushed through, his arm twisted behind his back by the man who had left earlier in a fit of rage. Jack has a large angry red mark on his face; there is a trickle of blood at the corner of his mouth; his coat and pants have scuffmarks and his hair is wet, snow clinging to him like he has crawled up out of an avalanche.

"Looky here what I found wandrin' around outside." The man speaks like a teenaged hoodlum showing off a stray cat to his buddies before tying a gasoline-soaked torch to its tail. "Now, what do ya think o' that?"

Instinctively, Dave comes at him yelling: "What the fuck are you doing? Let him go! What is your goddamned problem?"

"Awww! Worried 'bout yer girlfriend? Didn't hurt her much. Why don't you come 'an take her from me. Watch me break her arm before you get here."

[Lights out. Curtain.]

10

Intermission

[House lights up.]

As the curtain closes, people in the audience begin applauding. At the moment lights come up, house management workers open doors to the lobby. Sprightly people at the back of the auditorium rush to the door to be first to the toilets or just to be first. Others further down the aisles watch and wait, their opportunities to get through the doors quickly dissipating. It is the old dilemma of purchasing tickets close enough to see and hear the actors and being punished for it by the long wait as elderly or other people who otherwise struggle with bodily movement make their way up the raked floor grasping the backs of seats or other patrons arms as they fight the gravity that would roll them down the aisle and deposit them against the face of the raised stage or orchestra pit.

I'm all for cutting old folks a break. It's some of the others I find myself wanting to push aside so I can get past them. What is it with people who have no intention of going to the lobby but feel it necessary to stand in the aisle and won't step aside for others? I'm okay with people who remain in their seats or stand in front of their seats and stretch as long as they let other people get past them first. Some of the younger people climb over seats to the empty rows above them so they can avoid the waiting. I guess it's not unexpected that they would do such things. It's just not classy, but as long as they don't walk on other people's coats or drag the coats out of the chairs or step on the people sitting in the seats, it's not the end of the world. On the other hand, it strikes me as a rehearsal for who they'll be when they grow up. I get most annoyed with those people who push to get into the aisles and then block traffic from both directions while they carry on conversations with people they obviously don't see often enough outside the theatre.

"Excuse me," I say as I try to forgive their obliviousness about human beings other than themselves. Most of the time, a polite request doesn't seem to register with them, so I say it louder and with a bit of annoyance in my voice, "Excuse me!" Sometimes, I get lucky, and the person or persons will say, "Oh! Sorry," and move closer to the seats. Unfortunately, many times, I get the "Oh! Sorry" response and the conversationalists move two inches closer together, giving me and all of the people behind me an additional four inches of space to work with, but we do the best we can, turn sideways, suck in our stomachs, try not to touch bodies as we pass ... it's better than a fist fight, I guess.

In the lobby, people line up at the doors to the toilets. I feel particularly sorry for the women waiting to get inside to the always too small room with inadequate numbers of stalls. Standing in the lobby after five minutes of making my way up the slope to the doors with all manner of bodies bumping against me, I watch the pathetically slow progression, knowing there can't possibly be enough time for all of those women to get in and out before the second act begins. Undoubtedly, a man did the planning for the bathrooms and the space in the lobby where the women have to stand in line hugging the walls and blocking various doors and hallways that people are trying to get to. It's amazing how many times I see the women checking their cell phones or watches, looking forward and backward at the sloth-like movement of the line. The men's lines, on the other hand, move like candy in PEZ dispensers in the hands of an ungovernable child. Men are channeled into a chute and pushed mechanically in and out of heavy oak doors when a turnstile would have been more appropriate and saved a few trees.

In other parts of the lobby, people gather in little clusters to peck away at their perceptions of the play, to make polite conversation, or simply to hang out as they swallow the seeds of their own discontent while significant others make nice talk about their newly painted living rooms, ball games, TV shows, or the latest affair in which some prominent citizen is believed to be engaged. Occasionally someone says something about the script, the acting, the set, but not many. "I like," "I hate," "Not my cup o' tea," "I like the drunk," "Enjoying it," "It has its moments," "They talk too much," "It's depressing," or whatever other form of meaninglessness that passes for conversation. From my point of view, the best that can be said of all the inanity is that no one is coming through the front doors with AK-47s.

Perhaps I have lost all perspective, or maybe I just don't like reality. As I look at the crowd, I find myself lonely. Tired. Disconnected. Confused about my being here—the how and the why of it. My desire to escape the ever-increasing noise of the chicken coop overfilled with chickens takes me back through the auditorium under the light of the chandelier hanging high above the space. It hurts my neck to look up at it. I wish I could lie down in the aisle and stare at it for a while, preferably lying diagonally across the carpet so no one can get past me without stepping over, but I suppose that is a petty way to get even with the ignoramuses of the crowd and undue punishment for those who still maintain a shred of concern about others. Settling for a crick in my neck, I look up for as long as I can and accept that I am getting old.

Before me is the Grand Drape—the red wall that stands between the audience and the actors, the audience and the playwright, the audience as a mass of voyeurs taking part in the production of their own lives.

For a moment, I take comfort in the many shades of warm blood red of the drape. I wonder if anyone else thinks about the tremendous heft of it, the destruction it could cause if its half-ton load fell all at once uncontrollably from the rail upon the actors below like politicians without scruples falling upon the fears of others, clerics falling upon congregations to fund lies to beget more funds for more grandiose lies, like corporations falling upon humanity to fund the greed of their boards and their stockholders, like black upon white and red and yellow. But then, why should they think about a drape or any of the mechanical aspects of the theatre. They have come for something else.

A young, handsome Black man walks quickly down the aisle toward his seat in the center section of the theater, second row. I watch him move like an athlete, self-confident, comfortable in his body. He is smiling and I wonder about him—his life, his negotiations with the world he lives in. I have lost my place in the theater, crawled within myself, let imagination blind me, pull me inside myself to the sounds of gunshots in the far distance of my memories; I hear the crack of the knot at the base of skulls as bodies drop; I hear the cussing of grown men mutilating a 14-year-old Emmett Till. I hear the hatred of the men dragging people out of their homes in Tulsa in 1921. And Slocum, Texas; Colfax, Louisiana; Wilmington, North Carolina; Elaine, Arkansas; and on and on and on. I feel myself cringing, and I want to go to where that young man sits and tell him I am sorry. I am sorry for all of it! But I have no way of knowing that he is troubled by such things or that he would welcome my using him to assuage my guilt or my singling him out as others in surrounding seats listen to my lame attempts to say something of any consequence as I make him a stand-in representation of all oppressed people.

Sorry is the land and time I live in. I am sorry that Confucius, Abraham, Siddhartha Gautama, Jesus, Muhammad, Joseph Smith, Lord Krishna, and others, have not saved us, that they have not stepped into the spotlight of fame to perform the plays they wrote for themselves. Yet, despite their failures, their words continue to pluck the strings of discordant lutes trying to coerce the world to accept them for both good and ill. Though they linger, they are the old men of enlightenment and spirituality. Now they compete with the followers of capitalism, socialism, communism, republicanism, fanaticism, imperialism, militarism, fascism, Nazism, paganism, favoritism, nepotism, and on and on into multitudinous variations of these and other inclusionary/exclusionary doctrines—each version claiming some superior status, correctness, or worthiness for controlling people who are desperate to give up all personal responsibility—each of the "isms" offering survival, success and/or wealth while deliberately deemphasizing the standard two-point font of clarification at the bottom of their promotional material that says: "DISCLAIMER. Rules may change without notice at the discretion of those in control. If you don't pay, you can't play. No guarantees whatsoever."

It's tempting to think of destruction. But then that niggling hope thing that I have—many of us have still—throws a tarp over my rant, makes me want to think of this time in our history as a wall to be dodged around, climbed over,

tunneled under, or knocked down. I hear the thoughts falling like dust out of my brain, "Stay focused on the work!"
"Get through this. At least get through the second act."

The woman who had been sitting immediately in front
of me has returned to her seat, and I fear that I will have
to ask her once again to remove the wide-brimmed hat
that blocks sections of the stage from my view. It's a mas-
terpiece of obstruction. Its long yellow silk scarf is wound
into a band to hold sprigs of plastic flowers. I think of Scar-
lett O'Hara on screen, though I read somewhere that the
styles used in the film were historically inaccurate. Maybe if I were to tell the woman what I had read about the
movie's costuming she would be embarrassed enough to
remove it and stuff it under her seat. Then again, what do
I know about hats? How do I know she is trying to be Scar-
lett? I am certain there is plastic fruit on it—ala Chiquita
Banana—somewhere in the midst of the flora, maybe fau-
na too: a rabbit or cute little skunk hiding behind a plastic
tree trunk waiting for the right time to run down the tuxe-
do tails of that scarf—tails that I am sure extend down her
back, under the seats and out the emergency exit. Maybe
I am exaggerating a bit, but this is what it feels like sitting
behind her. I keep hoping she will remove it of her own
accord. She didn't take it well when I asked her prior to
the first act. She rolled her eyes toward her husband who
was diligently focused on pretending to be busy with his
cellphone, something more important than getting into a
fist fight over her stupid hat. She grudgingly removed it
while making the heavy breath sounds of exasperation. I

couldn't catch whatever she had said as she slapped the hat down on her lap.

The auditorium lights blink twice. I keep hoping she will remove it without my asking. When she doesn't, I ask her politely, sweetly, good-humoredly, "I am sorry to ask, but will you remove your hat? I hate to be a pest, but I can't see beyond it." This time, she turns her head to her side, looking back over her shoulder, more at the toxically perfumed old lady sitting beside me than to me, and says, "Too goddamn bad. Find someplace else to sit. I'm not taking it off." There is a part of me that wants to rebel, wants to tear the hat off her head and fling it like a Frisbee across the room in hopes that someone will catch it, throw it on the floor and stomp on it, but then I feel a pang of guilt at hoping someone else will finish the job that I know I won't start. I spy an empty seat against the wall two rows down and move quickly to get to it just as the lights come up and the curtain slides open and the people who have to turn their knees sideways or stand to let me pass show me their disapprobation in dirty looks, grunts, and crusty sighs, even as I say over and over, "I'm sorry. I really am sorry."

***

[Meanwhile ....]

Coming off stage at intermission, the actors toward the stage right exit. They are silent like monks going off to prayers. At the bottom of the stairs, Matt steps to one side, presses his back to the painted cement block wall, his head falling forward as he catches it between the palms of his hands. Reacting, Kevin lays his hand on Connor's shoulder, asks if he is all right.

"A bit of a headache. I'll bc fine."

Kevin squeezes the muscles of Matt's upper arms. "You were brilliant out there!

Brad has moved to touch Matt as well and repeats Kevin's sentiments before taking him by the arm and saying, "Come on, Matt. Let's get you into your dressing room so you can rest for a few minutes."

At his dressing table, Matt looks into the mirror at the images of the two men standing behind him and apologizes to their reflections for worrying them.

"I didn't realize how afraid I was to go out there tonight. It just overwhelmed me. I just need to rest.

"I suppose you think we're going to buy that bullshit, Matt?" Brad says. "You were brilliant, but you know goddamned well you're playing with fire. We smell the alcohol. You don't need that. You are too good an actor to give in to that."

Tears come into his eyes as he looks at the other actors' images in the mirror."

"You're right. I was scared and I drank. I won't do it again. Please don't tell anybody."

"Do you think we want to see you get canned? Kevin asks. We're not telling anybody. But are you going to hold it together for the second act ... no more drinking from here on out?"

"I will. I won't let you down. You guys go ahead with your own stuff. I need a few minutes to myself ... to beat myself up a little bit ... get my head together for the second act. I won't let it happen again. I promise." With that, he goes about the task of busily checking makeup until each of the men put their hands on his shoulders as a show of support before leaving him. Then, the door closes.

"I'm really worried about him," Brad whispers as he and Kevin get into the hall. "I hope to hell he is going to come through. It's one of those things you hope never happens: an actor who can't come on for the second act. I have a recurring fear that someday I'm going to be onstage waiting and I'm out there trying to find things to do or say that make sense and praying that the understudy isn't sleeping in the hallway and is ready and is on the way."

"I hear you. Improv can only go so far before you're writing a new script on the spot with consequences for everybody in the show. But it's all going to work out, Brad. He came through big time in the first act. He'll do it again. This has got to be tough for him. Everything'll be fine. You'll see."

"I hope you're right. By the way, I read your card."

"I meant what I said."

"I know you did."

When the call for "Places" comes, Brad and Kevin meet at the open door of Matt's dressing room. Matt isn't in it. They look up and down the hall and its tributaries, and then check the bathroom. In a moment of panic, they run up the stairs to where the stagehands are and tell one of them to let the manager know there might be a delay until someone finds the missing actor ... and they might want to make sure the understudy is ready just in case. As the young woman talks into her cell phone to inform the stage manager, Matt comes up the stairs with a smile on his face, confident, apologizing for being late. He winks at the other actors. As he leans forward to touch them, reassure them, they smell the vapors of alcohol rising out of his mouth. Before they can stop him, Matt has turned and is practically on top of the stagehand who is still talking with the stage manager and giving her his apologies as she turns her head from the alcohol saturated breath and states into the phone, "He's been drinking."

The actors move to the stage. The understudy stands backstage totally unaware that tomorrow will be the beginning of a whole new life.

11

Act II, Scene I

[Lights up. Curtain up.]

(As the curtain opens, we hear words from Act I, "Why don't you come over here an' take her from me and watch me break her arm before you get here. Dave stops abruptly, and the characters are in the positions they were in at the end of Act I.)

Dave Singh feels his muscles tightening, his focus sharpening, his brows shifting tightly toward his nose, his fingers folding into his hands, his knuckles protruding. It is only for Jack's sake that he doesn't lunge at the man physically, that he uses words thrown fast like gun blasts as a substitute for his instincts to attack.

"What in the hell is your problem? What do you want from us? Let him go!"

"I came to teach you queer boys a little lesson. Some respect."

Jack, trying to absorb the pain in his shoulder speaks rapidly, his head turning to his side and upward toward his captor, "We respect you, man. Didn't I tell you I wanted to be just like you?"

"Shut up, Asshole!" Turning to the bartender, he says, "Why don't you just pour me a shot of Jack, on the house, and bring it right over here to me. Even better, how 'bout you take off that stupid mask and bring the whole bottle of Jack over here, and then we'll talk about letting this asshole loose."

"Hey, I'd be happy to buy you a drink if you let me go," Jack says.

"Didn't I just tell you to shut the fuck up?" He puts more pressure on Jack's arm and moves him toward a table while keeping his eyes focused on Dave's reddened and intense face.

"Ow! Right. Sorry. I'll shut up."

Loudly ... speaking authoritatively ... demanding, Dave says, "I'm getting it, don't hurt him!" He pulls off his mask, throws it aside without thinking or caring about where it might go. When he gets behind the bar, he starts to bend down to get a glass.

"What the hell you lookin' under there for? Whiskey's behind you. Don't even try any hero shit, or I'll break him in half."

Straightening up, Dave shows his hands, turns, and lifts the bottle of Jack Daniels off the shelf. "Thought you might want a glass. Sorry."

"Just bring that bottle over here, Boy!"

The two men size one another up.

One barking orders, the other grudgingly complying— the controller and the controlled: the state of humans in general amidst the clashes of ideas about how the world is to work. Republican vs. Democrat; Christianity vs. non-Christianity; the State vs. the will of the people; freedom vs. authoritarianism ... all forms of black/white, either/or and win/lose. To bastardize Robert Frost's famous line, I hear in my head, "Something there is that doesn't love serenity!" Always, someone or something to overcome, someone or something to blame for the "is" that exists in any given moment in a life, something in our genes we carry from one generation to the next that fears the capabilities of the species.

There is a theory that we are essentially on a path to somewhere we—those of us living at this moment in time—cannot foresee because we cannot predict the minute changes in our genes that continue to alter the species for as long as the species survives. With enough alterations over eons, who knows whether those changes will be for good or ill? Will it matter one way or the other? Who knows? The concepts of good and evil may be lost altogether along the evolutionary path to that which might be or once was. So much depends upon the concept of hope and hopelessness that ride together in the red wheelbarrow of our existence.

Dave is careful to stand on the opposite side of the table from the man who is lifting Jack's arm up against his shoulder blades. Pain enhancement forces utterances of "ow," "unh" and "ughhh," to keep Dave at bay and keep Jack from trying to talk. An occasional, "Shit, Man," from Jack reacting to the pain gets through to make the man smile tauntingly at Dave as the bottle clunks against the Formica top of the table, but still in Dave's grip.

"I've brought you your whiskey. Now let him go."

"Tell you what. I'll let 'im go, if you sit down in that there chair and watch me drink your whiskey."

Jack interrupts, "Don't do it, Dave. He's going to hurt you." *[The man wrenches Jack's arm again.]* "Ow. I know, I know. Shut up."

"That's enough," Dave says. "I'll do it!"

Dave sits down still holding the bottle and then pushes it toward the man, but not far enough. The man leans forward to pick it up, his body off balance as he tries to reach around Jack to get it. As his fingers touch the bottle, his body shifts. His iron grip on his victim's wrist pulls Jack's arm downward. Jack takes advantage of the reduction in pain and the thug's lack of balance and twists away. Fumbling for control the man loses his grip all together, falls against the table, pushes against it to get himself upright. Dave is coming at him from around the table. Furious, the man kicks a chair onto its side, stopping Dave briefly as it slides several feet across the floor. The man's face is bright red with rage as he comes at and lands a powerful right cross on Dave's jaw sending him reeling momentarily

while he—the enraged man—tromps across the floor toward the bar where Jack has run. However, before the man
has gotten slightly beyond the table, he is stopped by the
barrel of the shotgun Jack has pulled into position.

"Stop right there! You're going to stop right now, or I'm
going to blow your head off!"

Dave, recovering from the blow has moved quickly toward the bar, avoiding the gun and staying out of the man's
reach. All action stops for a moment as the man looks at
Jack's dark and angry eyes. Stunned, Dave looks back and
forth at the two men waiting for one of them to blink. Believing he has only three choices—comply, fight, or die—
the man kicks the table hard enough to knock the open
bottle off of it, its contents spilling out as it rolls over the
edge to the floor without breaking, making sounds no one
hears as the whiskey continues to spill out on the floor.

Shouting, his voice shaky from the fear that had risen
inside of him, Jack says, "That's it! You take another step in
any direction and you're dead!"

And then it is over; the contest has been decided by the
gun and the determination on Jack's face as he looks down
the site line aimed at the man's chest.

The man's hands rise up in front of his chest, palms
out to suggest compliance.

"Whoa! Whoa! Come on. Let's calm down there, Buddy." The man's voice has become one of pleading, one far
less menacing than it had been when he was in control.
As he takes in his position standing on the other side of
power, he starts to manufacture the voice of reason, a

willingness-to-compromise voice, an I-was-just-kidding voice, a let's-be-friends-now voice that might have worked were all the participants eight years old.

Jack was angry, speaking loudly, his eyes threatening, "Calm down? Calm down? You about break my arm, disrespect Dave's property, you come in here with all your shit-for-brains hatred and wanting to hurt people for no reason, you beat me up and you punch my friend in the face, and you want me to calm down?"

"No reason for anybody to get killed here," the man responds.

"You mean no reason for *you* to get killed!"

"Come on! You ain't the kind of guy who's gonna wanna kill somebody. Come on. Put that 'ere gun down."

"I'm a guy now? You don't know anything about what kind of guy I am. If you so much as twitch wrong, you might just find out."

Dave interrupts, "We need to get the police here."

"Yeah, Dave," Jack responds. "We've seen how that's been working out!"

Jack is feeling the trigger, the hard steel, the giver of life and death against his forefinger. He is feeling what he thinks is pleasure –the pleasure of squeezing into a state of hyper-masculinity so acceptable to many men, "the justifiable use of force"—coerced cooperation and resolution. Absolute power to make others conform to the dictates enforced at the open end of a barrel, "winning" for once. The idea holds briefly until the thought of self-destruction rises up in his consciousness. Conscience wraps a hand over his nose and mouth to smother his desire to squeeze the trigger; it wipes away the image of hiding the carcass of destruction in a dark corner behind a flaming hearth of guilt that he knows he will wear every day of his life here- after and into his coffin at the end of his life. He feels his hand shaking as he straightens his finger and holds it off to the side of the trigger assembly and watches the sweat gathering on the man's face.

"Tell you what! How about I just walk out of here and we just pretend it never happened, Okay? How about that?" The man is becoming more panicky.

"But it did happen. And now you just want to walk away, and we're supposed to forget about it until you come back with some of your buddies and try to kill us?"

"That's not gonna happen. Just let me go, an' you'll nev- er see me again. Come on. I promise."

Using his best rendition of a police officer's voice, Dave steps closer to Jack and says to the man, "Seems to me we've got ourselves a bit of a mess here. At the moment, I see two choices for you. My friend here blows a hole in you the size of one of my tables, or I call the cops, and they come haul you off to jail for assault and battery and whatever else the law might dream up for you." [He turns toward the bar.] "What do you say, Jack?"

"I'd rather not have to fill out any paperwork or have to show up in court for his trial. Option one is less hassle in the long run." A gleam of mischief has returned to Jack's eyes as he quickly looks aside to Dave and then returns steadfastly to the duty of the gun.

"Come on, Guys. You don't need to do either of those things. Let me go, and I swear you won't be bothered again."

Dave looks at the man, and then at Jack, and then back at the man and says, "You know, I don't think my friend here believes you. Tell you what! How about you just get yourself down on the floor face first and stretch your arms out in front of you? I think my friend here's pretty worked up, so I wouldn't advise you trying to do anything stupid."

"Come on. You don't want to do this."

"We didn't want any of this," Dave says. "You wanted it, and now you don't like how it turned out."

Jack tries to match the authoritative voice as he says to the captive, "Just keep remembering the first option. You know, the part about the hole the size of the table in your gut."

"Okay. Okay. How about you call those cops and have them come pick me up?"

"How about you do what I asked?" Dave is eager for the danger to end, for the man to become less a threat, for Jack to be safe. He reminds the man of what he wants him to do. He directs him step by step, watches as the man goes down on his knees while still holding his hands out in front of him in surrender mode.

"Okay. Okay! I'm doing it. Don't let him shoot me."

"All the way down on your stomach, hands straight out at your sides." Though he doesn't take his eyes off the man on the floor, he walks out into the space to stand just slightly away from the man's work boots, then speaks to Jack:

"Jack, you come out here and keep your eye on him. I'm going into the back room for a minute."

"Believe me, I'm watching him. I'm just hoping he is stupid enough to try something." As he is talking, Dave is moving quickly toward the backroom. He opens the door and disappears momentarily while Jack aligns the bead of the gun with the man's back.

"Come on, man. You've got me. I don't wanna be shot. How about you call those cops?"

"How about you just lie still so my trigger finger doesn't twitch?"

"You got it, Man. I'm not moving. Don't shoot me."

Dave comes out of the backroom carrying a roll of duct tape and says to Jack, "You keep that gun pointed right at him." Speaking to the man on the floor, he says, "Now, Mister, I'm going to take your hand, and you're not going to move. Got it?"

"Just do what you gonna do. Just don't let him shoot me!"

"That's all up to you, Buddy." Dave pulls the left hand up off the floor and wraps two layers of duct tape around the wrist. He motions for Jack to come up beside him while he straddles the man, folds the fastened wrist and arm against the man's back. "Now slowly fold your other arm back. I would advise you to be very careful not to make my friend here think you're not cooperating. You never know what might set him off." The man complies. Dave brings the hands together back-to-back and wraps duct tape around both wrists at least five times. Dave tells the man not to move; he gets up and moves to the man's lower legs. "Now bend your knees and put your lower legs up in the air." When the man complies, Dave squats and wraps layers of duct tape around the ankles. "Okay, Jack. I believe the serpent has been defanged. You can take the gun off him for a minute." "Better check him for weapons."

Dave frisks him from behind, pulls out the man's wallet, throws it onto a nearby table. He finds nothing else in the back pockets. "Okay. Let's pick him up."

When they get him to a standing position, they check his shirt and then move to check the pants pockets, patting them with their palms. There is a jackknife in one pocket and a set of keys in the other. Jack reaches in placing the back of his hand against the man's thigh while he scoops the knife out and puts it in his own pocket. Dave removes the keys, looks at them and returns them.

"What? You not gonna cop a feel now you got me where you want me?"

"Did you want us to?" Jack asks. "Sorry, Man. You're not my type, and even if you were, we would both have to want it."

"Mister," Dave says, "I don't know where you get your ideas, but believe it or not, that idea is disgusting."

Words slip out of Jack's mouth haphazardly: "And, sorry to tell you this, but you're not all that hot." Catching Daves eyes on him as he speaks, he tells himself it was unnecessary and wishes he could have sucked the words back into his lungs and let them dissemble there.

Holding the man in place, Dave tells Jack to grab a chair. They ease the man down into it. Dave wraps duct tape around the man's chest and the back of the chair. Then he wraps more duct tape around the man's ankles and weaves it back and forth between the front legs of the chair to keep them from moving in any direction more than fractions of an inch.

"What a' ya gonna do with my wallet?"

"Not interested in your money, Bud. Though you do owe me for the whiskey. I am interested in your driver's license."

"Are you gonna call the cops or just gonna keep me trussed up like a hog?"

"Haven't decided yet."

Jack can't resist asking, "Do they—whoever they are—truss hogs with duct tape? I thought they just slit their throats." Seeing the fear in the man's face, he feigns sincerity and says, "Don't worry, Buddy. Probably won't go that far." He watches Dave going through the wallet, pulling out the license, and laying it on the table and taking pictures of both sides with his cell phone.

"Go ahead! Let's get this over with! Call the cops so I can get out of here."

Dave turns toward the man. He is looking downward at his phone, moving his thumbs to swipe and click. When he is done, he puts the phone into his pocket and looks directly into the man's eyes as he speaks.

"How about we have a talk, William? What would you like me to call you: William, Will, Bill, Mr. Hagerty, or something else?"

"Now, what're me an' you gonna talk about? Just call the cops. I ain't talkin' to you. I'll wait for the cops."

"You're making an assumption we're going to call them, William."

"Aww. Come on. Whatta ya want?"

"A talk. That's all, William."

"Bill! I go by Bill. So ... whatta ya wanna talk about?"

"Bill, I want to talk about you."

Jack has picked up the gun again and is standing directly behind the captive. He watches Dave's face and demeanor and is trying to assess where this "talk" is going. Obviously, the question has manifested itself in his face and Dave is reading it and wants to reassure him: "How about you have a seat where you can keep an eye on him, Jack? *(He points to a chair.)* And keep that shotgun handy just in case."

"How about—first—you and I talk for a minute over there?" Jack is pointing to a space near the entrance door. Nodding toward the man, he says, "I don't think he's going anywhere." Gun in hand, he takes Dave's arm and walks him to the space and asks in a whisper, "What do you think is going to happen here, Dave? You think you're going to talk him out of being who he is? Turn him around, get him to confess his sins?"

Matching Jack's level of whispering, Dave responds with, "I don't know. I just don't want to be as awful as he is.

Where the hell does all of this stop? I'm just tired of all the anger, people hating one another. I don't know what I want. Maybe I just want to understand why he hates; maybe I would like to find a reason to let go of my anger at him and other people like him, find a reason not to hate."

"You know he kicked my ass outside a little while ago; he punched you in the face. I'm not seeing a lot of good in this guy at the moment."

"I get it. For a minute there, I wanted to do some punching of my own for what he did to you; I wanted to get even. But that's my point. We're all so busy getting even that there's no way to stop. Maybe all I can do right now is slow it down with this one angry man just for a short while. But isn't that better than nothing? What happens if we all just stop trying?"

"You're a better man than I am, Dave. I'll go along—against my better judgment—but if I don't see something that changes my mind in this talk of yours, I'm pressing charges. Let's make it clear this isn't a free ride. I want this guy out of here, and I don't want him coming back."

"I'm with you. I don't want him back either." He pauses briefly, looks at Jack's face growing redder and puffier, feels the ache in his own jaw. "You're likely to have a hell of a bruise, Buddy. By the way, quite a performance back there with the gun! If you're not careful, I could learn to like your company."

"Looks like I need to get a little less careful then. And, by the way, you're not coming out of this without a bruise of your own."

The two men return to their prisoner. Jack lays the shotgun on a table approximately six feet from Hagerty. The gun barrel is pointed toward the thug and the butt is within a few inches of Jack's hand when he sits down. Dave pulls a chair directly in front of the man, sits down, their knees nearly touching.

"So, say whatever it is you're gonna say, so's we can get this over with," Hagerty demands.

"I already told you, Bill, I want us to talk together, you and me, like real people.

"How am I supposed to talk like real people when I'm strapped down and can't move?"

"How are we supposed to talk when you're not strapped down and you're trying to beat the shit out of us? This is the middle ground, Bill. Best I can do for now. How about you tell me a little bit about yourself?"

"Whatta ya mean?"

"What kind of work do you do? Hobbies, stuff like that."

"Who gives a shit?"

"I assume your family does ... assuming you have one. I would really like to know."

"Mechanic. Hunting. I like hunting."

"Oh, yeah? What kind?"

"Deer. Turkey. Why would somebody like you care? You aren't the hunting type."

"That's not fair, Bill. I've hunted. My dad was a hunter all his life. I went out with him most of the time I was growing up. Then one day I didn't like it anymore. But I respected hunters even after I decided it wasn't for me.

I've stood out in the woods late at night many times with my father waiting for the coonhounds to "tree" a raccoon. Ever do that, Bill?"

"Not my thing."

"Did you hunt with your dad, Bill?"

"Sometimes."

"Did you like being with him?"

"I don't wanna talk about that fuckin' asshole. You a shrink or something?"

"No, Man. I'm just talking. My dad wasn't what anyone would call a perfect father; I just said he took me out hunting. Not very kind to my mother or his kids. Mostly ignored us until he decided we needed strict discipline. He was good at punishment. Only other thing he had any passion for was hunting. By the time I was a teenager, there was almost nothing left between us."

"Why're you tellin' this?"

"I don't know, Bill. Maybe I thought you and I have something in common; that's all. How about wife and kids? Have any kids, Bill?"

"Leave 'em out of it. Why you asking me these dumb-assed questions. Just call the cops."

"You don't like being held like this, not being in control?"

"What the hell do you think?"

"Kind of seems to me like what people like Jack and me feel a lot of the time."

"You ain't nothin' like me."

"Why? Because I'm gay?"

"That's right."

"You ever been hurt by a gay person, Bill?"

"Not until now."

"Have we hurt you?"

"Not yet. Got me trussed up though."

"Why do you suppose that is?"

"Cuz you got the drop on me."

"Did we track you down, come into your home and "truss you up," as you say, because we didn't like you?"

"No."

"So, how did you end up in this situation?"

"Look! Ya got me. Call the cops. I don't wanna play this game."

"You just hit the nail on the head, Bill. You called it a game. But it isn't a game. People get hurt, go to jail, go to war, get killed, everybody hating everybody, and happiness is way off in the distance where none of us can get to it ... and here we are. How do you think you ended up here, Bill?"

"I was pissed and came back here, and you hood-winked me—two against one."

"So, we made you angry?"

"Yeah. You an' all your goddamn rules about masks and what I can watch on TV an' you makin' a goddamn fortune off people with your high prices." Nodding toward Jack, "An' smart-ass there thinkin' he's so much smarter 'n everybody else. An' don't think I didn't know he was makin' fun of me neither. I'm not as stupid as he thinks.

Jack interrupts, "I don't think you're stupid. I just don't get what it is you want or why you have to be so goddamned meanspirited about people who haven't done a goddamned thing to you except try to live on the same planet."

"Whatta ya mean ya don't get it? I'm just sick and tired of everybody gettin' a break 'cept us hard-workin' white men in this country. Women, nig . . blacks, fags ... everybody but white men!"

Dave interjects himself again when he sees the agitation on Jack's face, "So, you feel like the deck is stacked against you and other white men?"

"Goddamn right! And it ain't a feelin'; it's fact. Just call the cops and let me out of here?"

"Can I ask you a tough question, my friend?"

"I'm not your friend! An' I don't see as I have any choice in you asking whatever."

"Do you like yourself? I mean deep down, do you like who you are?"

"What kind of faggy-assed question is that? Men—real men anyway—don't go around thinkin' 'bout shit like that. I'm not gonna answer that. What the hell is this, a church meetin'? You waitin' until I break down an' cry? Ain't gonna happen."

"No. Not a church meeting. Just some men sitting down and talking to one another. At least, I was hoping we might talk. It looks like you're not really into talking. Here's the thing, Bill: you have chosen to hate us, and there's nothing I can say or do to convince you not to, but, you know what? I'm choosing not to hate you. I'm just sorry you can't see that neither Jack nor I deserve your hatred. We're not taking anything away from you or anyone else.

We're just trying to live our lives, same as you. You don't like that we're different from you. That's okay, but how are we hurting you? I used to believe that any two people or groups of people should be able to sit down and reason out how they can get along together ... but, I guess that's really impossible unless both sides want it or are at least willing to try making it work. You're not there. So, probably best to end our conversation."

"Then what? You gonna call the cops? What you gonna do? You're not gonna let this guy shoot me. Right?"

"I want to tell you something and I want you to listen: I hate how you came in here and dissed my place and most of all, my friend here." He points to Jack. "We have every right to press charges against you, you know? And I can't control what Jack does. He's a full-grown man, just like you, and he can choose to hate or forgive. I can't control him. I don't want to control him or you or anybody else. I hope he doesn't shoot you. I'm asking him not to. But that's his choice. He might go ahead and press charges whether I do or not. He'll decide that for himself." He pauses for a moment, looks at Jack and then turns back to the man, saying, "I am truly sorry that you hate me, and I'm even more sorry you hate Jack. He's a good man. I don't like what we had to do to be safe around you. You left us no choice but to protect ourselves just so we can live in the same country you think is all yours. And even though you deserve whatever the law might throw at you, I'd like to ask Jack if he would be okay with us letting you go."

Jack has guessed that this would be the outcome of the talk. Dave's words have been working on his mind, convincing him that he too could be a better man if he tried. He reminds himself that he said he was giving up hate, and yet, the thought is challenged by the aching in his face and the soreness that is beginning to spread along his back and legs from being thrown onto the hard ground. For a moment he vacillates between wanting revenge and wanting to be the kind of man he is finding Dave to be. When he starts to speak, he doesn't know for sure what he has decided, but he is suddenly comfortable with seeing where the words take him. When he speaks, it is like writing a character into a passage because he needs to be there, not knowing what is best for him to say until he's said it so at least there is something for the writer to start working on.

He talks directly to Dave, "There's a part of me that would like to kick his ass for the beating he gave me, but you're right. It's not going to make anything better. It might feel good for a minute; but then I have to live with myself afterward. I don't want to hate this guy. I just wish to hell he could figure out there is room for all of us."

The man's eyes dart back and forth between the two younger men: hope to the left, fear to the right and incredulity in the space between them. "You're serious? Really? You're gonna let me go?"

"Yeah," Dave responds. "We're serious. But we're also not stupid. I took a picture of your license on my cell phone. And I sent it to some of my friends. They're Jack's friends too. They know both of us and watch out for us. And now

they know who you are too. I've sent one to the police department too and told them you've made threats and that
if anything happens to either one of us at any time in the
future, you are the first person they should go after. So, you
just might get a visit from the cops one of these days, and
you'll have to figure out how you want to handle that."

Then he turns to Jack and says, "You might just want to
pick up that gun and come over here and watch our friend
while I cut him loose, just in case he wants to try doing
something stupid again."

"I'm not gonna do anything, I promise. You'll never see
me again."

Dave goes to the bar, returns with a pair of scissors,
and kneels down in front of Hagerty to cut the duct tape
that has held his ankles fast.

"I want to believe you, Bill. I really do."

"You don't have to worry."

When he has cut the tape from the ankles and chair
legs, Dave moves to the back of the chair, cutting the tape
that has held the man's chest and back against the wood
spindles. Finally, cautious to stay to one side of the captive,
he cuts the tape at the man's wrists. Groaning, the man begins to stretch his legs, feels the blood flowing more freely
in his veins, feels the ache of his body to change position,
and pulls at the tape scraps still attached to him. As Dave
moves to stand alongside Jack, he takes a moment's pleasure in thinking of his friend as a caricature of a TV cowboy,
gun in hand and ready at a moment's notice to do what a

man has to do for what's right for the womenfolk and children when the law was nowhere to be found.

When he rises, the man—Bill Hagerty—looks at them and the barrel of the gun Jack has lifted to chest height, moves cautiously to the table where his billfold has been sitting. He checks to see that his license is back in its place behind the yellowing plastic sleeve, and then he thumbs quickly through the bills before realizing even if he had been robbed—which he hadn't—there isn't much to be done about it when any complaint might be met with a shotgun blast. Wordlessly, he turns and starts out the door, but before pulling it shut, he stops like an old man who can't remember why he has come into a room. And then, like that same old man, he suddenly remembers and takes a couple of steps toward the first table. Jack is raising the shotgun. The man reaches into his back pocket, fishes a twenty-dollar bill out of the leather billfold and drops it on the table. "For the whiskey ... Can I have my knife back. *[Jack pulls it from his pocket and tosses it to him.]* The door bangs against the doorframe as the man walks through the door, up the sidewalk past the windows, and out of sight.

Rushing forward to assure himself it is over, Jack, watching the man climb into a jacked-up red Ford truck and driving away, says into one of the front windows, "Bye, Bill! Have a good life!" Then he and Dave look at one another, the tension dropping off their bodies like hot summer sweat. The whiskey bottle that Bill had knocked to the floor lay wet and sticky—a something to be attended to, something to do when there is nothing for Dave to do but process the experience. He goes to the remnants of destruction with a determination to restore his creation— his space— assesses what will be needed. When the assessment is done, he assembles the tools: a roll of paper towels, a small bucket filled with soapy water, and a cloth for mopping. In the meantime, Jack has found the broom and dustpan and swept up the broken O'Doul's bottle.

Dave sets the bucket on the floor just beyond the whiskey spill that has been spread widely by the broom that removed the glass shards. He gets down on his knees, dips the cloth in the water and starts wiping up the mess, mopping, wringing, mopping, until he can get the space clean enough for a clear water rinse. Between the moments of scrubbing and wiping floors, tables, chairs, and carrying the water bucket (washing and rinsing) back and forth, he is bantering with Jack:

"You know, Jack, old Bill was right about one thing for sure."

"What's that?"

"You are a smart-ass!"

"What about you and the hardball cop routine?"

"I guess I've watched too many cop shows. I didn't need to make anything up, it was just there when I needed it. And what about you and the macho-man shotgun routine? How'd you even know exactly where it was?"

"Saw it when I was chasing your stupid basketball around."

"I told you! It's not a stupid basketball. I'm marketing the game. Going to make a fortune off it."

"Right! Pad of paper, a jar, and a roll of tape."

"People made money off Pet Rocks!"

"That's true."

"Think you could've shot him?"

"I was hoping to hell it wouldn't go that far. I was really afraid he was going to kill one of us. Maybe both of us."

"You ever used a gun of any kind?"

"No. But I've seen them on TV."

"Did you know that gun wasn't loaded?"

"Seriously? Not loaded? What the hell good is it then?"

"Guess you could hit somebody over the head with it if necessary. You sounded convincing. Scared the shit out of him."

"Why do you keep it?"

"It was the one my dad gave me when I was a boy; I just can't make myself get rid of it. You remember in the old movies when the bartender always had a gun behind the bar? I just thought it was funny."

"But what if somebody stole it and used it in a crime?"

"Won't do them much good. I had the firing pin removed, and the barrel is filled with epoxy. Like I said, I keep it because my father gave it to me ... only thing he ever gave me other than his anger. Serves a purpose, I guess. I used it to get you to pay up and you used it to save us from getting killed."

"Did you really send the pictures of that guy's license?"

"Yeah, I did."

"To the cops?"

"I suppose I could have tried sending it as a text to their main number."

"So, you lied."

"He didn't know that. Which reminds me, I better call the cops and let them know about this just in case Bill decides to come back." Dave pulls out his cell phone and presses the speed dial. He is waiting for an answer.

"And, that wasn't the end of your little web of deception!"

Dave raises his free hand, palm out toward Jack and says, "Hold on!" then speaks into the phone, "No, not you! I was talking to someone else. This is Dave Singh again, Dave's Place. Yes! I need to make a report. No, don't hang up ... it's about one of the guys I told you about before. Did you find him? I'm worried about him. I hope you're right. No, whole new situation. A threat. I know I told you a guy made a threat before, but he came back. No, not the drunk. The guy that wouldn't leave. No that's a different situation. No. He's gone now. Well, I still want to report it just in case. No. I don't want to press charges. I just want it on the record. No, he's not walking around the streets. That was the drunk. He drove off in a truck. No, not the drunk. The second guy. You know what? I'll come down to the station tomorrow and talk to somebody then." The sound of Jack's laughter has penetrated Dave's consciousness, and he starts to laugh though he tries to maintain his normal voice as he finishes his conversation with the person at the police station. "Thanks for your time. No, I won't call again. I hope. Okay. Okay. Bye."

"I'm surprised they aren't sending someone out to arrest you for annoying the hell out of them tonight," Jack says through his laughter.

"Them? Annoying them? What about doing their jobs? I'm worried about our banker friend; by now he could be frozen to death. Somebody needs to do something!"

"You reported it! What else can you do? You know, Dave, you've got some silly notions that people do things because they are right things and because right things need to be done. For most people, right things get done when there is money to be made in doing them, my friend."

"You're a cynic."

"I might be a cynic, but obviously not a good one. I went along with you on releasing Bill. Remember? I'd like to think people can be reasonable, can make decisions based on what is good for other human beings as well as themselves and that people can do good if we give them a chance. I really wish it were like that; I really do. I wish people didn't hate one another. I wish people would sit down and talk their way through problems, but I'm sorry to tell you this, that's not the way the real world seems to work. People—not all, but many, many—are incapable of deep reasoning, seeing other people from any point of view other than their own, or dealing with facts that conflict with their superstitions and ridiculous beliefs. Much of the world runs on the power of bullshit, Dave; it's full of inept people just stumbling through their lives doing what is easiest and requires the least amount of brain power."

"But there are also a lot of people who see the potential for making it better. Should we stop trying to make a dent in stupidity?"

"No, of course not. But people like you and me, Dave, we can't make people be the way we want them to be any more than they can make us into what *they* think all people should be. They have the right to be stupid if that's what they want to be even after getting through our education system. It's kind of like what I was telling you about my dad. Sometimes we've just got to accept people for who they are and live our own lives the best we can."

"Stupidity is dangerous, Jack. And the only thing I know how to do is keep trying to get people to let us be who we are and learn that they can be okay with that."

"You should have been a teacher, Dave. By the way, Mr. Decency and Honesty, you told our buddy, Bill, that your friends are my friends, and they care about us both. I don't know your friends, and they don't know me. You don't even know where I live, what my phone number is, or what my email is, let alone sharing any of that with your friends. Deception, Buddy!"

"Quick reminder here, Bucko! You were ready to kill a guy with an empty gun! A deception. Except you didn't know it at the time. Yes! I lied. I didn't exactly have time to introduce you to my friends. The lie may have saved our lives."

"Lies didn't save us from getting our asses kicked and our faces punched. I think I'm going to have a shiner in the next day or two."

"It'll make you even more macho than you already are. You can tell everybody you went toe-to-toe with a man twice your size, and he came out of it worse than you did."

"I like that."

[Lights out.]

12

Act II, Scene II

[Lights up.]

(The room is straightened up except for two tables pushed aside. Dave and Jack are taking outside shots at the mug with paper wads–"Basketballs." They are razzing one another about missed shots and interference, calling "cheating" on one another. After a moment, Dave stops and checks his cellphone.)

"**O**ne-thirty. Not looking like we're going to get any customers. What do you say? Shall we call it a night?"

Disappointment slips into the pauses between Jack's words as he responds. "I guess. ... Sure. Can I ... can I help do whatever you do for closing?"

"You know what? I'm just going to shut things down, check a couple of things. Everything else will be fine until tomorrow. You want anything before we go?"

"You mean like a nightcap? No. Told you I'm not much of a drinker. I like the concept though, might use it in a story, but not into it for myself."

"I've just got to go into the back room, check the back door and the coolers, turn off some lights. I'll be right back."

"Sure, boss."

As Dave leaves, Jack picks up the bottle he has been nursing and starts towards the bar. As he gets to the bar, he hears the sound of the door opening and turns to see the banker come in. He is unsteady, his clothes wrinkled, shirt tails out.

Seeing him, Jack shouts, "It's you! We've been worried about you." Surprised at his own feeling of relief, Jack's first instinct is to yell for Dave, give him the news that the prodigal son has come home at last. The banker is trying to get his coat off, struggling with extracting his arms from the sleeves and struggling to maintain balance.

In a muffled inarticulate slurring of words, the banker asks, "Why worried? I'm here. Where else would I be?" Walking toward Jack, he has managed to get the coat off, one sleeve pulled inside out; he drops it haphazardly on the edge of a table where gravity starts pulling it toward the floor. Stepping forward and catching it, Jack lifts it and pushes it into the heap the banker had started—a more balanced heap away from the table's edge.

"We were looking for you!"

"Why?"

"We were worried about you!"

"Why?"

"You disappeared from the back room. We were afraid you'd die out in the cold."

"Do I know you?"

"We sat here and talked, remember?"

"Don't know what you're talking about?"

"Okay. Maybe you forgot. You were here earlier."

"I was?"

"Yes."

"Don't remember."

"We were trying to get you home, but you wouldn't tell us your name."

"James Lathrop. Why wouldn't I tell you my name?"

"I don't know. Wouldn't tell us where you live either."

"With my wife."

"In Willett? Is she there now?"

"Think so. Haven't checked. She threw me out. Need a drink."

"The bar is closed for the night. We were just locking up." As Jack is talking, lights behind the bar and in the hallway leading to the bathrooms go out.

"See? The lights are being turned off."

"But, you're here! How about a nightcap?"

He reaches into his pockets, and a wad of crinkled bills falls out around his ankles. "Oops. Dropped my money."

Jack responds as he bends over to help the man with the money that has fallen to the floor. "Not tonight. Do you have a way home?"

"Call a cab."

"You want me to call one for you?"

"No. Staying with my sister next door. Not going home."

Struck by the sudden revelation of why the banker had disappeared, Jack says, "Aha! Next door! ... Sounds like a plan. You go next door to your sister's and get some sleep."

"Just came from there. ... How 'bout one for the road?"

"Like I said, we're closing up. You should go back there."

As Jack hands the stacked pile of bills to Lathrop, the banker says, "Ah, you keep it."

"Thank you. But, no. I can't." He forces it into Lathrop's hand.

"Your loss, Buddy."

"You never know, Mr. Lathrop. You just might miss that money when you sober up." He picks up the coat, fixes the sleeve and holds it for the man to slide his arms into.

When Lathrop, with Jack's help, has pulled his coat into place, he says, "More where that came from. Got plenty. Pile at my sister's place."

Laughing, Jack says, "Did you go and rob that bank of yours, Mr. Lathrop, or did you rob your sister?"

Lathrop uses the hand stuffed with money to press his pointer finger over his lips and sputters, "Shush, you!" His eyes grow dark as the skin on his forehead wrinkles, his eyelids close to slits where the eyeballs had been. The green of the money seems to have penetrated his skin making him suddenly sinister. He stuffs the money into his coat pocket, and as he does so, the darkness that had come over his face fades away, returning his image to his former chalky flesh and the drunk's half smile.

"Okay! Well, you have a good night then, Mr. Lathrop!"

"How? Everybody hates everybody. Haven't you heard?"

I wish you a good night anyway ... and for whatever it's worth, I don't hate you Mr. Lathrop."

"All right, young man! I'm leaving. You have a good night. I forgive you."

"Thanks. But what am I being forgiven for?"

"For not giving me that drink."

"Thank you. Now, go and sin no more."

(The banker leaves.)

Dave comes out of the backroom as the banker walks past the window and says excitedly, "That's the banker. We've got to stop him."

As he starts moving forward, Jack tells him to stop. "I talked to him. He was in here looking for a drink. He's staying next door at his sister's place. That's why we couldn't find him. He's fine. I think he might have robbed his bank or his sister or he's just plain stinking rich. Told me he's got lots of cash at his sister's house, so much that he wanted to give me a bunch of it. I had to force him to take it back. By the way, his name is James Lathrop."

"You think he stole the money? Maybe we should call the police."

Pleadingly, Jack speaks loudly, "God! Please. No. I don't think we can go through that again. Do it tomorrow. We know where he is."

"You're right. If I call them again, they'll come lock me up."

Dave goes behind to the cash register and turns the lock key and puts the key in his pocket before he turns and pumps plunger of the hand sanitizer to get the gel in his palm and works it into his skin. He slides the bottle toward Jack as an offering like bread on the table for the last supper.

Taking a clean, white cloth from under the counter, he wipes the bar while waiting for Jack to finish rubbing his hands dry. "So much for dodging the Covid stuff, huh? Breathing in the fumes coming off customers, having to handle them close up and personal. Lot of good the masks did! Hope neither of us pays a price for it."

"I hope not too. But I have to say it's been a hell of an adventure."

Ritualistically, Dave continues to touch the resurrection of wood, keeping its skin clean so the blood veins of its history will survive, protected from the hands of indifference and willful destruction.

Watching Dave, his radiating sense of connection, his moment of being lost in the love of this beautiful thing he resurrected from the graveyard of antiquities, Jack understands for a fleeting moment what it means to be loved. "You did a good thing, Dave. You saved it. You made it beautiful again."

"When I touch it, it gives me hope."

There is a brief pause as the two men look into one another's faces. "Time to leave, huh?"

Dropping the cloth behind the bar, Dave grabs his coat from the storage room behind him and switches the overhead lights off, leaving only the faint light of a street-lamp to enter the room and the path to the door.

At the darkening of the room, struggling with his emotions and suddenly irritated, Jack speaks loudly.

"Just like that, Dave? Time to leave? ... I don't want to just leave like this. Weird as it sounds, I've had one of the best nights of my life meeting you. We had something going, I thought. And you just want to leave like it was nothing?"

"Did I say I was leaving without you?"

"Well, no, but you didn't say you were leaving with me, either."

Dave walks up to Jack, wraps his arms around him, looks into his eyes and then kisses him tenderly. "You know what they say about assuming, Jack. Your place or mine?"

(Interior light fades almost to black. Exterior light rises creating a silhouette of a large man who steps into the space between the light and the door, a shotgun rising from his side as he prepares to kick the door open.)

[Lights out. Sound of door crashing. Curtain.]

13

Curtain Call

[Lights up. Curtain opens.]

B rad Michaels walks on from stage right; Kevin Lane comes from stage left; and Matt Connor comes from center stage and meet at the stage apron—a synchronized effort to please the audience one last time in appreciation for their applause and bow before them in unison. They hold hands and raise their arms together over their heads accepting appreciation for the ensemble performance and the work of all those behind the scenes. Each of them knows that the applause must be taken as it comes and the actors have to sense exactly the right moment for leaving, the moment of greatest impact on the audience, letting them go home feeling good but still wanting more, and the moment of greatest impact on the actors as they begin to think about moving on, getting out of the theater, unwinding, going out to celebrate or going home.

At that magically appropriated time the actors break their handholds, wave to the crowd and walk single file offstage. And it is done. The mantle of joy begins to fall immediately from their faces as they feel the weight of exhaustion coming over them, the inevitable sense of loss that comes with spending the energy that has been pulled from places the actors had not known were within them, the fears of having to live up to or improve upon their own standards night after night for weeks to come.

As they make their way to the bottom of the stairs and open the door to the painted concrete walls of the basement hallway, three producers and the director walk out of Matt's dressing room door. The director is holding a pint bottle of Wild Turkey in his hand. His eyes fix momentarily on Matt, who is moving guiltily toward him. The director shifts his gaze to the two younger men, and he and the producers shout words of praise, "Bravo," "Great Job," "Fantastic Work," and they applaud, but they do not look into Matt's eyes again. They smile at Kevin and Brad as they motion for Matt to come into the dressing room, each losing his smile as he steps inside. The door closes hard behind them.

"I don't want to be in my dressing room right now," Brad says. "Walls are too thin. Can I come down to your place for a few minutes? I want to talk to you anyway."

"My place?" ... "Oh. You mean my dressing room." Kevin smirks as he looks at Brad.

"For now," Brad says, smiling.

As they walk to the other end of the hall to Kevin's dressing room, they talk quietly as they wonder what is happening with Matt.

"I smelled the alcohol every time I got near him. But I've got to say, he was phenomenal out there tonight, a hell of a fine actor. Better half-drunk than some so-called actors I know when they're completely sober."

"Maybe they'll give him another chance, give him a break ... maybe."

14

Epilogue
January 6, 2022

(The Fool Awakens in the same position as he was at the end of the prologue.)

Sobering, Matt Connor finds himself awake. His head hurts. His stomach is sour. There is but little moisture in his mouth to spread with his tongue upon his dry and cracking lips. His body stretches itself out of the fetal position he has taken. Through swollen eyes, he looks out into the seatless, once-was auditorium at large pieces of fallen plaster strewn across the floor like the debris of Berlin's Trinity Church after the bombing. On the side wall a poorly drawn swastika with disproportionate lines has been spray painted in black, the paint so heavily applied that it has rolled like blood from a wound off its arms.

He rolls onto his back, looks up at the patchwork of plaster clinging by tiny hair fibers to dry, gray lath still intact on parts of the sloped ceiling designed to hide three tiers of lighting instruments ... light guns that once shot their rays upon the stage ... catwalks, and crew people who made special effects from on high. Fine silty dust hangs in the air—the grated product of minute shifting of the joists and rafters moved by fractious winds and breezes, rain and snow breaking through sections of the rotting roof and by time's determination to destroy ever so slowly. Some of the dust has settled upon his body during the hours he slept. He looks up into the space above the stage where rails once flew, where magic had fallen from the sky gently and quietly through the hands of crew members waiting for their cues while they stood in the narrow walkways that led to the rigging. All of it gone: the heavy metal ladders, the walkways, the safety rails, the ropes, and the tons of counterweights. Now, only the course layers of un-pointed bricks remain, and they, too, are pocked not only by time, but by the efforts of workers and vandals picking the bones of the dead to release salvageable metal.

He rolls over slowly and painfully onto his knees and faces the opposing wall—the opening to the house—door-less. Beyond it, the shambles of a lobby where people once gathered to await the opening of the house and to be escorted by well-dressed men and women to the now ghosts of furniture numbered by section, row, and seat. Dim lobby light of broken windows lays in the openings like dead men. High above the doors, is a half-wall; the upper half, once glass covered, behind which stage and light management sat, calling and executing cues: lights, sound, curtains, fly-ins, fly-outs ...

In the far-left corner of the wall is another doorless opening, this one lightless. Had there been a door, it would have had a tasteful plaque saying, "Staff Only." Behind that door would have been the stairs leading to the control booth and to the Phantom's realm above the audience, above the ceiling joists, the mystical realm of surprise lights, confetti dropping, fog dumping, rain making and such, and any number of sounds that could be pushed through wires hung like spiderwebs to the amplification speakers now long gone, leaving behind them only the amplification of the building's last desperate gasps before dying.

With great effort, Connor presses his palms against the stage floor and struggles to raise his torso and get his feet and legs to raise him to a standing position. He waits for the feeling of lightheadedness to fade before he walks to the apron's edge where he remembers a time when he would have jumped the five feet down to the auditorium floor, taken pleasure in his body's agility and grace. Now, his only means to get from the *here* of the stage to the *there* of the house floor is to sit down, roll onto his belly, and slide off, and hope he will not to fall down as his weight forces him to connect with the bottom of the orchestra pit. As he slides free of the apron, his head hits the facing of the stage, causing him to cry out; however, he maintains the ability to stay upright. Unsteadily, he walks through the auditorium to the back wall and to the narrow opening that had once given access to the magical phantom's realm.

The first few stair treads are missing. Black holes of unknown depths have taken their place. Beyond this point he can see almost nothing except a faint light at the top edge of the stairwell where the staircasing ends and the catwalks—if they still existed—would have begun. Not knowing how sturdy the stair structure might be, he carefully places his right foot on the treadless riser where it meets the side of the wall. Pressing his hands against the narrow well of plaster and lath to lighten the weight of his body, he steps up. When he feels the rigidity of the riser's wood beneath him, he pulls his left foot up to the other side of the stairwell. Step after step, he carefully tests and lifts himself until he steps onto the platform at the top of the stairs where a small hole in the roof has let a trickle of morning light through.

As his eyes adjust, he sees numerous small rays of light hitting the surfaces of joists and the backside of lath strips with dried plaster that had oozed up between them long ago when the building was made. The space is largely one of joists, rafters, and cross bracing devoid of any means for traversing them easily. Each joists' wood—rough-sawn, thick, and hard—sits on its narrow edge alongside its mates, its broadsides facing one another, encouraging one another to carry the massive weight above and below— neat equidistant rows. Moldy plaster hangs from their collective bellies out of habit more than need. The rafters are propped above them like whale bones bearing the weight of an ancient sagging skin. A few scraps of wood and metal lie about. Here and there a few bolts and collars from which the catwalks hung remain fastened into the wood. It is a wasteland that time has brought to the inevitable immolation, demolition, or deconstruction of human constructs.

In his first attempt to find his way across the expanse of parallel lines, he steps off the platform, placing his right foot on the first narrow joist. As he lifts his left up to join it, he loses his balance and falls across a half dozen of the hard-edged joists, plaster beneath him breaking loose and hitting the floor thirty feet down like tiny bombs hitting their targets and dust shooting upward from the point of impact like a man's final breath.

The collision of his body against the unforgiving wood creates shooting pains throughout his body. He feels the trickle of blood down his forehead, the stabbing in his chest where his ribs had hit, the pain in his knees. And still he is determined to go on, pushing through his pain, moving across the joists one by one on his hands and knees, wincing as sharp edges of time-hardened wood press like knives against tendons and thin skin. When he reaches what would have been the center of the auditorium below—the place where the grand chandelier would have hung, he kneels on a joist, reaches across to the next to brace himself while trying to release some of the pain from his knees as he looks down through the opening, remembering the elegant ambiance of spaces such as this, the chandelier so brightly lit; its faceted crystal teardrops dancing above the people as carefully masked bulbs pushed their light against them like fine summer breezes playing tricks on the eyes of the patrons as they thumbed through their playbills—some oblivious to its light as art and too content with it merely as a means of cuing silence and intermissions—sitting down or standing up—a means for seeing who is present and what they are wearing.

One of the inset steel cross braces that kept the fixture from falling out of the sky remains just off to the side of the opening. It is thick in his grasp and unmovable as he tests it for its rigidity and strength. It will do. He feels the tears beginning to fall out of his eyelids, running down the dust on his face, dripping off his nose and chin and over the dried blood streaks made by the gash on his forehead. The tears begin to fall through the chandelier hole, and he begins to sob. He pushes against the rigid metal bracket, and then the joists until he rises to a near-upright position. He tries once again to control the balance of his body on the three-inch wide surfaces of two joists while he sobs into the palms of his open hands. His upper body begins to free fall out of his control; his legs are buckling; he drops once again, his knees and hands catching the surfaces of parallel joists. The scream of pain spills from his mouth. His chest hurts from convulsions of emotional exhaustion as he mutters, "Why?"

After a few moments of staring down through the opening, he unbuttons his sweat-soaked shirt, pulls the tails out of his pants and drags the wet cloth away from his skin. He uses it to wipe the sweat, salt, dust and grime from his face. It takes several swipes to stop the stinging of the salt around the cut on his forehead. It takes time for his vision to clear. When it does, he ties one sleeve of his shirt to the hard-steel bar—that one remaining brace that had held bejeweled elegance in its time, held that creation of a sun that once lit this house. He wraps the other sleeve around his neck and ties it in a double knot and lowers his body into the space between the joists, the lath groaning and cracking beneath him.

He looks at me through red and dripping eyes, his lips quivering as if a last question is about to break ... but it does not come. He brushes away the stray fly buzzing at his face, instinctively brushes the spot on his brow where it had touched, then wipes under his eyes and waits ... as do I ... as do we all.

www.ingramcontent.com/pod-product-compliance
Lightning Source LLC
Chambersburg PA
CBHW022032120726
47899CB00007BA/2384